THE GAM

Now, match [...] [co]n-sulting detectiv[e ...] [do]n't completely suc[ceed ...] [it mig]ht be wise to keep in mind Holmes' advice to Watson and all would-be detectives:

"It is an old maxim of mine," he said, "that when you have eliminated the impossible, whatever remains, however improbable, must be the truth."

Editorial Contributions: Kurt Fischer, Jessica Ney

Production: Terry K. Amthor, Richard H. Britton, Coleman Charlton, Kurt Fischer, Jessica Ney, John Ruemmler, Suzanne Young, Rob Bell, Karl Borg.

Sherlock Holmes was created by the late Sir Arthur Conan Doyle and appears in novels and stories by him.

Grateful acknowledgment to Dame Jean Conan Doyle for permission to use the Sherlock Holmes characters created by Sir Arthur Conan Doyle.

© 1987 IRON CROWN ENTERPRISES, P.O. Box 1605, Charlottesville, Virginia, 22902.

ISBN- 0-425-10607-1

All Rights Reserved.

PRINTED IN THE UNITED STATES OF AMERICA

Distributed by The Berkley Publishing Group, 200 Madison Avenue, New York, New York, 10016.

SHERLOCK HOLMES SOLO MYSTERIES™

THE BLACK RIVER EMERALD

by Peter Ryan

Series Editor: John David Ruemmler
System Editor: S. Coleman Charlton
Cover Art & Illustrations by Daniel Horne

B
BERKLEY BOOKS, NEW YORK

CHARACTER RECORD

Name: DAVID ROGERS

Skill	Bonus	Equipment:
Athletics	+1	1) NOTEBOOK
Artifice	+1	2) PENCIL
Observation	+1	3) PENKNIFE
Intuition	+1	4)
Communication	+1	5)
Scholarship	+1	6)

Money: 12 pence, 8 shillings, 4 guineas, 3 pounds

7)
8)
9)
10)
11)

NOTES:

CHARACTER RECORD

Name:

Skill	Bonus	Equipment:
Athletics	____	1)
Artifice	____	2)
Observation	____	3)
Intuition	____	4)
Communication	____	5)
Scholarship	____	6)

Money: ____pence
____shillings
____guineas
____pounds

7)
8)
9)
10)
11)

NOTES:

CHARACTER RECORD

Name:

Skill	Bonus	Equipment:
Athletics	_____	1)
Artifice	_____	2)
Observation	_____	3)
Intuition	_____	4)
Communication	_____	5)
Scholarship	_____	6)

Money: _____pence	7)
_____shillings	8)
	9)
_____guineas	10)
_____pounds	11)

NOTES:

CHARACTER RECORD

Name:

Skill	Bonus	Equipment:
Athletics	____	1)
Artifice	____	2)
Observation	____	3)
Intuition	____	4)
Communication	____	5)
Scholarship	____	6)

Money: ____pence
____shillings
____guineas
____pounds

7)
8)
9)
10)
11)

NOTES:

CLUE SHEET

- [ ] **A** _____
- [ ] **B** _____
- [ ] **C** _____
- [ ] **D** _____
- [ ] **E** _____
- [ ] **F** _____
- [ ] **G** _____
- [ ] **H** _____
- [ ] **I** _____
- [ ] **J** _____
- [ ] **K** _____
- [ ] **L** _____
- [ ] **M** _____
- [ ] **N** _____
- [ ] **O** _____
- [ ] **P** _____
- [ ] **Q** _____
- [ ] **R** _____
- [ ] **S** _____
- [ ] **T** _____
- [ ] **U** _____
- [ ] **V** _____
- [ ] **W** _____
- [ ] **X** _____
- [ ] **Y** _____
- [ ] **Z** _____

CLUE SHEET

- [ ] **AA** _____
- [ ] **BB** _____
- [ ] **CC** _____
- [ ] **DD** _____
- [ ] **EE** _____
- [ ] **FF** _____
- [ ] **GG** _____
- [ ] **HH** _____
- [ ] **II** _____
- [ ] **JJ** _____
- [ ] **KK** _____
- [ ] **LL** _____
- [ ] **MM** _____
- [ ] **NN** _____
- [ ] **OO** _____
- [ ] **PP** _____
- [ ] **QQ** _____
- [ ] **RR** _____
- [ ] **SS** _____
- [ ] **TT** _____
- [ ] **UU** _____
- [ ] **VV** _____
- [ ] **WW** _____
- [ ] **XX** _____
- [ ] **YY** _____
- [ ] **ZZ** _____

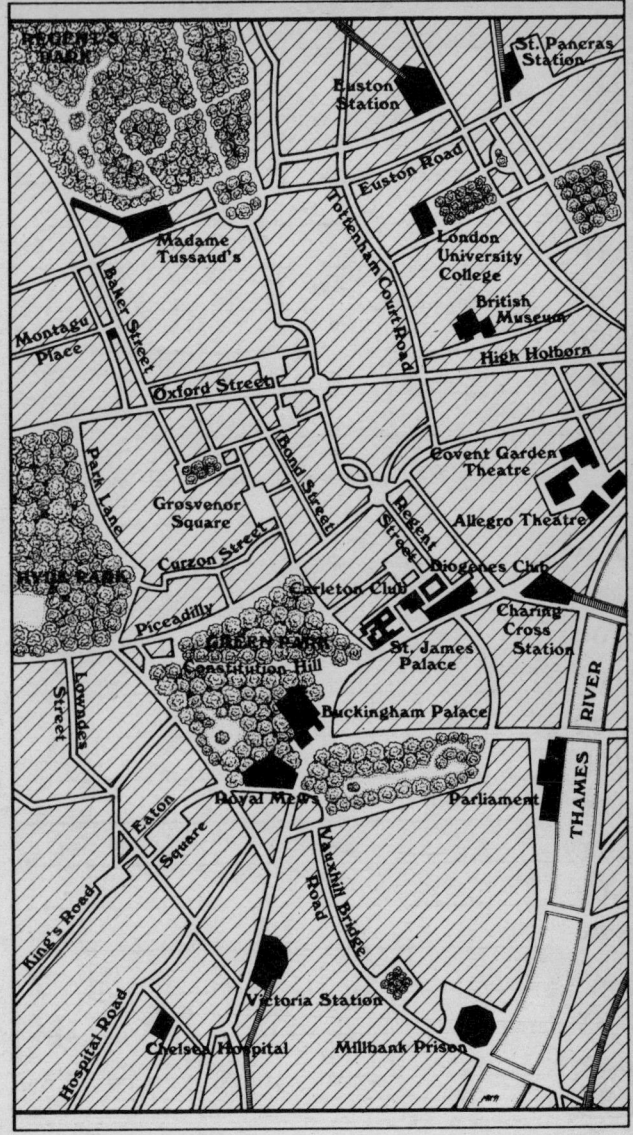

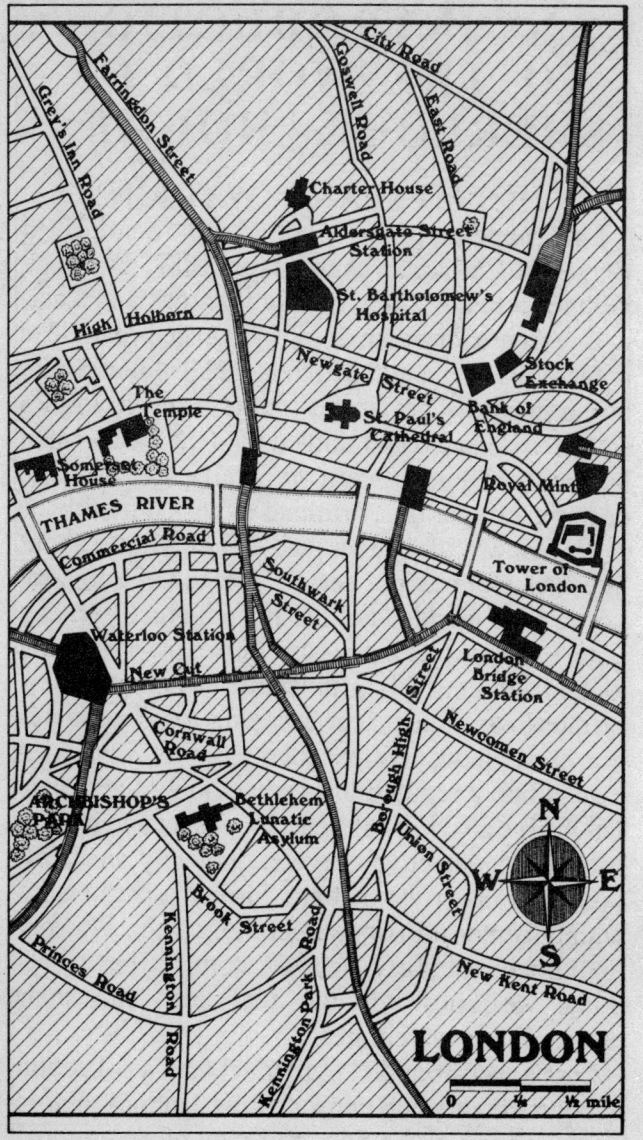

AN INTRODUCTION TO THE WORLD OF SHERLOCK HOLMES

HOLMES AND WATSON

First appearing in "A Study in Scarlet" in Beeton's Christmas Annual of 1887, Sherlock Holmes remains a remarkably vigorous and fascinating figure for a man of such advanced years. The detective's home and office at 221B Baker Street are shrines now, not simply rooms in which Holmes slept and deduced and fiddled with the violin when he could not quite discern the significance of a clue or put his finger on a criminal's twisted motive.

We know both a great deal and very little about Sherlock Holmes as a person. The son of a country squire (and grandson of the French artist Vernet's sister), Holmes seems to have drawn little attention to himself until his University days, where his extraordinary talents for applying logic, observation and deduction to solving petty mysteries earned him a reputation as something of a genius. Taking the next logical step, Holmes set up a private consulting detective service, probably in 1878. Four years later, he met and formed a partnership with a former military surgeon, Dr. John Watson. Four novels and fifty-six short stories tell us everything we know of the odd pair and their extraordinary adventures.

Less a well-rounded individual than a collection of contradictory and unusual traits, Holmes seldom exercised yet was a powerful man of exceptional speed of foot. He would eagerly work for days on a case with no rest and little food, yet in periods of idleness would refuse to get out of bed for days. Perhaps his most telling comment appears in "The Adventure of the Mazarin Stone:"

I am a brain, Watson. The rest of me is a mere appendix.

Holmes cared little for abstract knowledge, once noting that it mattered not to him if the earth circled the sun or vice versa. Yet he could identify scores of types of tobacco ash or perfume by sight and odor, respectively. Criminals and their modus operandi obsessed him; he pored over London's sensational newspapers religiously.

A master of disguise, the detective successfully presented himself as an aged Italian priest, a drunken groom, and even an old woman! A flabbergasted Watson is the perfect foil to Holmes, who seems to take special delight in astonishing his stuffy if kind cohort.

In "The Sign of Four," Holmes briefly noted the qualities any good detective should possess in abundance (if possible, intuitively): heightened powers of observation and deduction, and a broad range of precise (and often unusual) knowledge. In this *Sherlock Holmes Solo Mysteries*™ adventure, you will have ample opportunity to test yourself in these areas, and through replaying the adventure, to improve your detective skills.

Although impressive in talent and dedication to his profession, Sherlock Holmes was by no means perfect. Outfoxed by Irene Adler, Holmes readily acknowledged defeat by "the woman" in "A Scandal in Bohemia." In 1887, he admitted to Watson that three men had outwitted him (and Scotland Yard). The lesson Holmes himself drew from these failures was illuminating:

Perhaps when a man has special knowledge and special powers like my own, it rather encourages him to seek a complex explanation when a simpler one is at hand.

So learn to trust your own observations and deductions — when they make sense and match the physical evidence and the testimony of trusted individuals — don't rush to judgment, and if you like and the adventure allows, consult Holmes or Watson for advice and assistance.

VICTORIAN LONDON

When Holmes lived and worked in London, from the early 1880's until 1903, the Victorian Age was much more than a subject of study and amusement. Queen Victoria reigned over England for more than 60 years, an unheard of term of rule; her tastes and inhibitions mirrored and formed those of English society. Following the Industrial Revolution of roughly 1750-1850, England leaped and stumbled her way from a largely pastoral state into a powerful, flawed factory of a nation. (The novels of Charles Dickens dramatically depict this cruel, exhilarating period of sudden social change.) Abroad, imperialism planted the Union Jack (and implanted English mores) in Africa, India, and the Far East, including Afghanistan, where Dr. Watson served and was wounded.

Cosmopolitan and yet reserved, London in the late Nineteenth Century sported over six million inhabitants, many from all over the world; it boasted the high society of Park Lane yet harbored a seedy Chinatown where opium could be purchased and consumed like tea. To orient yourself, Consult the two-page map of London on pages 10 and 11. You will see that Baker Street is located just south of Regent's Park, near the Zoological Gardens, in the heart of the stylish West End of the city. Railway and horse-drawn carriages were the preferred means of transport; people often walked, and thieves frequently ran to get from one place to another.

THE GAME'S AFOOT!

Now, match wits with the world's greatest consulting detective. And have no fear — if you don't completely succeed at first, just play again! It might be wise to keep in mind Holmes' advice to Watson and all would-be detectives:

"It is an old maxim of mine," he said, *"that when you have eliminated the impossible, whatever remains, however improbable, must be the truth."*

Good luck and good hunting!

THE *SHERLOCK HOLMES SOLO MYSTERIES*™ GAME SYSTEM

THE GAMEBOOK

This gamebook describes hazards, situations, and locations that may be encountered during your adventures. As you read the text sections, you will be given choices as to what actions you may take. What text section you read will depend on the directions in the text and whether the actions you attempt succeed or fail.

Text sections are labeled with three-digit numbers (e.g., "365"). Read each text section only when told to do so by the text.

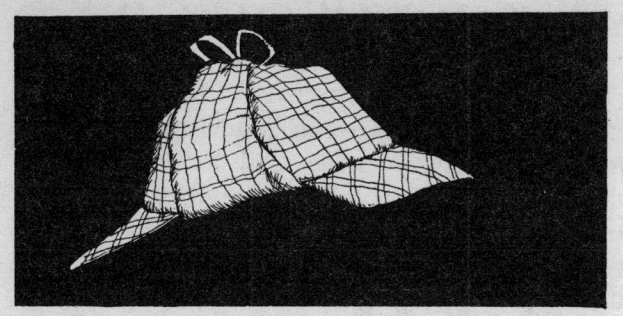

PICKING A NUMBER

Many times during your adventures in this gamebook you will need to pick a number (between 2 and 12). There are several ways to do this:

1) Turn to the Random Number Table at the end of this book, use a pencil (or pen or similar object), close your eyes, and touch the Random Number Table with the pencil. The number touched is the number which you have picked. If your pencil falls on a line, just repeat the process. **or**
2) Flip to a random page in the book and look at the small boxed number in the inside, bottom corner of the page. This number is the number which you have picked. **or**
3) If you have two six-sided dice, roll them. The result is the number which you have picked. (You can also roll one six-sided die twice and add the results.)

Often you will be instructed to pick a number and add a "bonus". When this happens, treat results of more than 12 as "12" and treat results of less than 2 as "2".

INFORMATION, CLUES, AND SOLVING THE MYSTERY

During play you will discover certain clues (e.g., a footprint, murder weapon, a newspaper article) and make certain decisions and deductions (e.g., you decide to follow someone, you deduce that the butler did it). Often the text will instruct you to do one of the following:

Check Clue xx or *Check Decision xx* or *Check Deduction xx.*

"xx" is a letter for Clues and a number for Decisions and Deductions. When this occurs, check the appropriate box on the "Clue Record Sheets" found at the beginning of the book. You should also record the information gained and note the text section number on the line next to the box. You may copy or photocopy these sheets for your own use.

Other useful information not requiring a "check" will also be included in the text. You may want to take other notes, so a "NOTES" space is provided at the bottom of your "Character Record". Remember that some of the clues and information given may be meaningless or unimportant (i.e., red herrings).

EQUIPMENT AND MONEY

Whenever you acquire money and equipment, record them on your Character Record in the spaces provided. Pennies (1 Pence), shillings (12 pence), guineas (21 shillings), and pounds (20 shillings) are "money" and may be used during your adventures to pay for food, lodging, transport, bribes, etc. Certain equipment may affect your abilities as indicated by the text.

You begin the adventure with the money noted on the completed Character Record sheet near the front of the book.

CHOOSING A CHARACTER

There are two ways to choose a character:
1) You can use the completely created character provided at the beginning of the book. **or**
2) You can create your own character using the simple character development system included in the next section of this book.

STARTING TO PLAY

After reading the rules above and choosing a character to play, start your adventures by reading the Prologue found after the rules section. From this point on, read the passages as indicated by the text.

CREATING YOUR OWN CHARACTER

If you do not want to create your own character, use the pre-created character found in the front of this book. If you decide to create your own character, follow the directions given in this section. Keep track of your character on the blank Character Record found in the front of this book. It is advisable to enter information in pencil so that it can be erased and updated. If necessary, you may copy or photocopy this Character Record for your own use.

As you go through this character creation process, refer to the pre-created character in the front of the book as an example.

SKILLS

The following 6 "Skill Areas" affect your chances of accomplishing certain actions during your adventures.

1) **Athletics** (includes fitness, adroitness, fortitude, pugnacity, fisticuffs): This skill reflects your ability to perform actions and maneuvers requiring balance, coordination, speed, agility, and quickness. Such actions can include fighting, avoiding attacks, running, climbing, riding, swimming, etc.

2) **Artifice** (includes trickery, disguise, stealth, eavesdropping): Use this skill when trying to move without being seen or heard (i.e., sneaking), trying to steal something, picking a lock, escaping from bonds, disguising yourself, and many other similar activities.

3) **Intuition** (includes sensibility, insight, reasoning, deduction, luck): This skill reflects your ability to understand and correlate information, clues, etc. It also reflects your ability to make guesses and to have hunches.

4) **Communication** (includes interviewing, acting, mingling, negotiating, diplomacy): This skill reflects your ability to talk with, negotiate with, and gain information from people. It also reflects your "social graces" and social adaptivity, as well as your ability to act and to hide your own thoughts and feelings.

5) **Observation** (includes perception, alertness, empathy): This skill reflects how much information you gather through visual perception.

6) **Scholarship** (includes education, science, current events, languages): This skill reflects your training and aptitude with various studies and sciences: foreign languages, art, history, current events, chemistry, tobaccory, biology, etc.

SKILL BONUSES

For each of these skills, you will have a Skill Bonus that is used when you attempt certain actions. When the text instructs you to "add your bonus," it is referring to these Skill Bonuses. Keep in mind that these "bonuses" can be negative as well as positive.

When you start your character, you have six "+1 bonuses" to assign to your skills.

You may assign more than one "+1 bonuses" to a given skill, but no more than three to any one skill. Thus, two "+1 bonuses" assigned to a skill will be a "+2 bonus", and three "+1 bonuses" will be a "+3 bonus". Each of these bonuses should be recorded in the space next to the appropriate skill on your Character Record.

If you do not assign any "+1 bonuses" to a skill, you must record a "-2 bonus" in that space.

During play you may acquire equipment or injuries that may affect your bonuses. Record these modifications in the "Bonus" spaces.

The Black River Emerald

Cast of Characters

Mark Avery: a student at Belton and owner of the emerald, given to him by his father.

Sir Richard George Bingley: Richard Bingley's aristocratic father.

Richard Bingley: student, formerly Mark Avery's best friend, son of a nobleman.

The Black River Indians: a tribe from the Amazonian jungle, they are the original owners of the Black River Emerald.

Becky Connoly: the pretty daughter of a local mill worker.

Joe Connoly: Becky Connoly's father.

Timothy Mahoney: a trader-adventurer.

Joe Miller: The village beggar and drunkard.

Karl Mueller: the headmaster of Belton School.

"Oxy" Oxfield: student at Belton and member of the Society of Five.

Ken "Muskrat" Rafferty: student at Belton, Oxy's sidekick, son of "Ratnose."

Mr. "Ratnose" Rafferty: thief and underworld figure.

David Rogers: a student at Belton School, accused of the theft of the emerald. The detective/hero ("you") of the story.

The Society of Five: a secret society of students at Belton School, inlcuding Mark Avery, Richard Bingley, Oxy Oxfield, Ken "Muskrat" Rafferty and David Rogers (you).

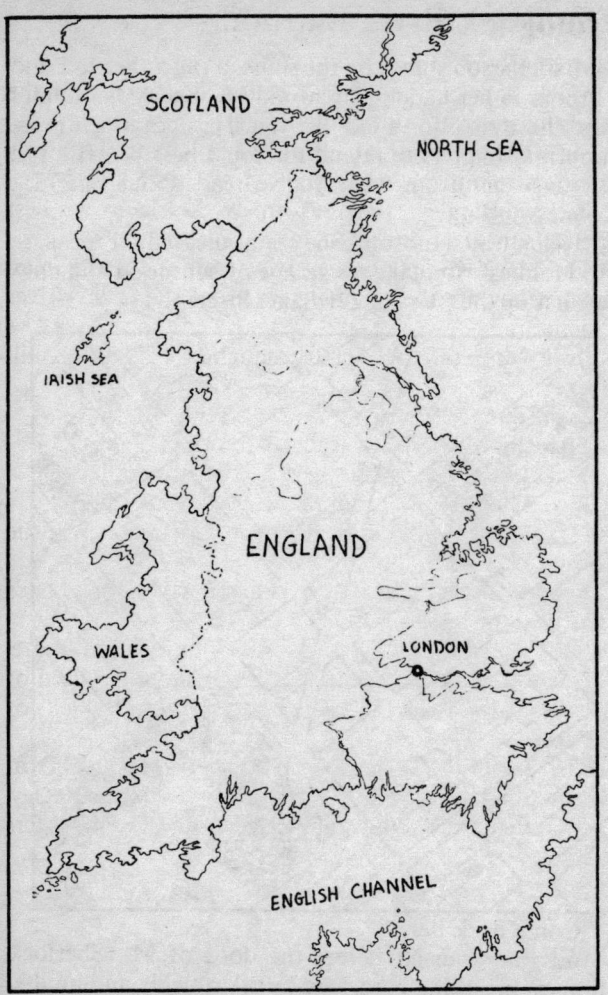

Prologue

Mrs. Hudson stands on the stairs, a rug at her feet and a broom in her hand. "I'm afraid Mr. Sherlock Holmes won't have time for a lad like you. He's got much more important matters to attend to. You'd best be off." You recognize her from what you've read about Sherlock Holmes.

"Hello, Mrs. Hudson." She seems pleased. "I must see Mr. Holmes." You take advantage of her mood and dash past her up the stairs of 221 Baker Street.

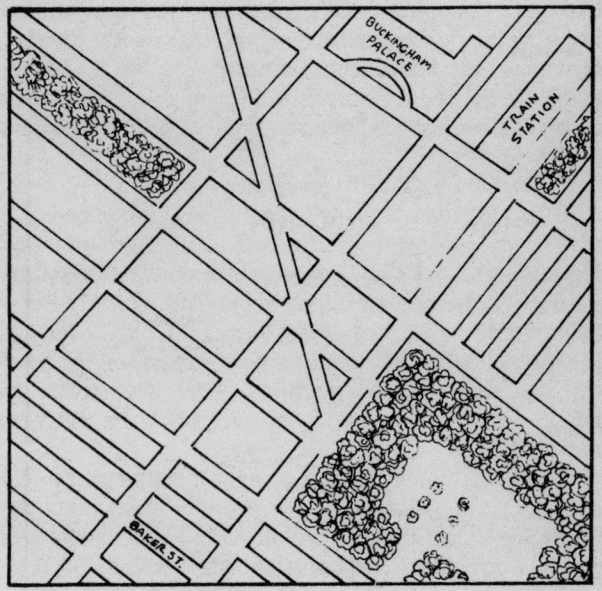

"Come back here!"

You find yourself before the door of Mr. Sherlock Holmes, breathing hard. You knock quickly and loudly. A pleasant-looking man in a suit and waistcoat opens the door, looking down at you.

"Yes?" he inquires, and you recognize him as well.

"Dr. Watson, I should like to see Mr. Sherlock Holmes."

"My dear boy, Mr. Holmes is presently busy on a case.

Not to be disturbed. The game is afoot! Perhaps if you'd leave your name and come back in a few weeks. Or perhaps" — he smiles modestly and rocks back on his heels — "I could help. I have solved a case or two..." He coughs modestly.

"I must see Mr. Holmes!" You dash past him into the room. Books litter the tabletops, shelves and floor. The spiral end of a violin juts out below the fading leaves of a manuscript. A bony hand grabs you by your suitcoat and lifts you into a chair beside the window.

"Well, who have we here?" You look up to see a beak-like nose, drooping eyelids, and grey eyes as bright and keen as rapiers, which gaze down at you intently. Sherlock Holmes lights his pipe and studies you. "A school-boy at Belton School in Shropshire. One of our cousins from across the sea, I should guess — an American by the name of David Rogers."

"Why, that's right!" you sputter, amazed.

"I say, Holmes, how the devil..." Watson exclaims.

"If I explain, you will find my deductions obvious," Holmes sighs. "The boy is wearing the uniform of a public school. The monogram BS on the pocket indicates Belton School, one of our great boarding schools, which has sadly fallen on hard times. His name is written on the inside of his coat, which I read when I lifted him. And as for being an American, well, his accent gives away his nationality."

"Well, of course," Watson replied, "that does seem obvious."

Holmes turns to you. "Tell me, have you come by some new found wealth? Or was this jacket a gift?"

"A gift," you tell him, amazed. "A gift from my best friend, Mark Avery."

"Holmes, I say!" Watson interjects.

Holmes raises his pipe. "What singular point do you notice about his clothes?"

Watson shrugs. "They seem to me like a typical public school uniform."

"You see, Watson, but you do not observe," Holmes notes. "The trousers are old and threadbare, while the shoes are worn to the peculiar diagonal in the heel that betrays a long history of walking pidgeon-toed. They exhibit the signs of considerable wear, as does the shirt. Notice the frayed collar and cuffs, and the cracked third button. But the jacket, Watson, is quite a different case." Holmes fingers your coat sleeve. "This wool is highest quality Merino lambswool from New Zealand — the softest wool in the world. The coat has a fine stiffness as well, which comes from camel hair blended with the wool. From the fibers I would guess Mongolian camel hair, from the coat of the two-hump Bactrian camel. And the tailoring, Watson, notice the intricate stitching, for which our tailors are renowned. There are, of course, a number of other details I could list, but this jacket is so distinct from his other clothes, and of such superior quality and condition, that he must have either been given it or have come into a small fortune to purchase such an item."

You feel the jacket sleeve before speaking. "I had no idea Mark had been so generous. He gave it to me for Christmas, because mine was coming apart. My parents aren't wealthy and can just afford to send me to the school. And Mark thinks I stole the emerald! No wonder he feels so bitter." Tears sting your eyes. "He was my best friend!"

"An emerald was stolen?" Holmes inquires calmly.

"It was Mark's father's. He had it locked in a strongbox in our room."

"Imagine!" Watson says, scoffing.

"Mark told me the stone was priceless, a rare jewel from an Indian tribe in South America or some place. And Mark blames me, he thinks I took it. But I didn't..."

"There, lad, we believe you," Watson says, putting his hand on your shoulder. "Holmes, the lad is at his wits' end."

Holmes lights his pipe. "Tell me, what is your roommate's full name?"

"Mark Avery."

"The Averys of Lockland Hall?"

"That's right."

Holmes frowns and goes to his shelves. He takes a thick volume from the shelves and flips through the pages. "Does the stone look like this?" To your amazement, he points to a drawing of very jewel that was stolen. Even in the picture, the jewel seems to gleam.

"Exactly!"

The legend under the stone reads: *The Black River Emerald*.

Holmes shuts the book and frowns. "So the Black River Emerald has been stolen." He takes a puff from his pipe. "Watson, if you'd be so kind as to look up the Black River Indians..."

Watson takes down a great volume, riffles through the pages, and hands it to Holmes.

"Black River...tributary of the Amazon...hum! Indians a warrior tribe...visited by Irish monks, 1856, and

1863-65...failed to convert, abandoned mission. Brought back tales of magical stone. Well, that's not a great deal of information." He closes the book and pulls on his pipe.

"Why the deuce did Mark bring the jewel to school at all?" Watson exclaims.

"He'd lost a foolish bet with one of the other boys in the Society, Richard Bingley. That was his end of the wager, to bring the jewel he was always boasting about, a treasure Richard claimed he had invented." *Check Clue MM*.

You pause before continuing your explanation. "If he didn't bring the emerald, Mark would have lost face with the others in the group and faced expulsion from the Society. It was particularly stupid, because there had been a number of thefts at the school recently — even another while Mark had the emerald at school. Of course the teachers and headmaster searched the school from top to bottom each time, but they couldn't find any of the stolen goods." *Check Clue XX*.

After a deep breath, you go on: "Anyway, his father indulged Mark; he adores his son. He let Mark bring it for just the month between Fall break and Christmas hols, which are coming up this Friday. We may seem like silly schoolboys to you, but the Society was the most important thing at school. I couldn't believe I got in, and I was only accepted because of Mark." Tears well in your eyes again, and you curse yourself.

"Holmes, I say," Watson exclaims, and puts a hand on your shoulder. "Reminds me of my old days in the Regiment. Nothing finer than friendship. Did I tell you how Jenkins and I — "

"Whom do you suspect?" Holmes interrupts briskly.

"Only five of us even knew about the jewel — the members of the Society of Five. Mark didn't want to publicize the fact of having a priceless treasure around."

You see on Holmes' keen, alert face a tightening of the lips, a quiver of the nostrils, and a concentration of his tufted brows. "Five, you say. Who are the five?"

"Well, Mark, of course, but he couldn't have been the

thief. He was the owner."

"Anything is possible, however improbable." Holmes says, relighting his pipe.

"And myself. And a boy named Oxy Oxfield. A great hulking bully, like his name says. I first thought of him. He was fascinated by the stone, as a child would be." *Check Clue OO*.

Holmes' eyes seem to burrow into your soul as you continue talking. "When Mark would bring the stone to our secret meetings Oxy would sit staring at the glow — this great hulking bully, who mauled you just for walking down the hall — all calm and quiet, like he was in a spell. And I can understand why, too; the stone seemed kind of magical. I tell you there was this magic kind of feeling that you had being near it."

"Mmm," Holmes murmurs, exhaling a wreath of smoke. "Who else was a member of the Five?"

"Oxy's best friend, Muskrat. But they had been quarreling over money. His name is Ken Rafferty. Muskrat, we call him, because he gives off this strange musky smell."

Holmes's eyes take on a hard glitter. "Where is this Muskrat Rafferty from?"

"Brighton, I think he told me. His father is very rich, in finance or trade."

Holmes chuckles to himself. "Finance. Trade. Well you could call theft and burglary that. Belton School must have fallen on hard times, indeed."

"Whatever do you mean, Holmes?" Watson wonders.

"I've met the lad's father, Ken Rafferty, once — at the other end of a loaded pistol. At least I would wager this Muskrat is the son, for Ken Rafferty, too, has the aspect of a rat — and that very peculiar smell. I know just what the boy here means. They must be related; I'd wager on that. Ken Rafferty is one of the most famous black market figures in Europe." *Check Clue PP*. "This case takes on a distinct interest."

"So you think Muskrat took the emerald?" you inquire.

"Leaping to conclusions is often the most misleading error for an investigator. Who else is a member of the

Five?" Holmes inquires.

"Richard Bingley. His father is a nobleman, Sir George Bingley."

"Of course, the Bingleys of Dunworthy Manor," Holmes says, growing animated. "A line which traces their nobility back to the War of the Roses. His great grandfather was a Baron of the Exchequer, and another ancestor was a Lieutenant General in the battles against Louis the XIV, I believe. Curious that the boy isn't going to Eaton or Harrow."

"He said it was a family tradition to attend Belton" you reply. "We heard rumors, though, that he'd been a 'bother' at several other schools. Richard was Mark's best friend before me. But they had a falling out — after both were in the Society — and are now very bitter toward each other. No one has ever found out what caused the fight."

Holmes taps his pipe. "So young Bingley too, had a motive." *Check Clue QQ*.

"You can cut the air between them with a knife, Mr. Holmes. We five are the only boys who knew anything about the jewel."

"Does anyone else at the school, other than the father, know he brought the jewel to the school? Anyone Mark might have mentioned?"

"Well, the headmaster, of course. Mark did tell the headmaster about the stone, in case something happened to the emerald."

Holmes appears keenly interested. "I see. What is he like?"

"The headmaster? Oh, I can't imagine Mr. Mueller —" you begin. But Holmes' strict glance brings you up. "Well, Mr. Mueller is not the best liked man at Belton. He is a thin old man with a hatchet face. There is something mean about him, Mr. Holmes. His nickname — the boys call him, well, 'Ironbottom.' "

"I see. And how was the jewel stolen?"

"Mark kept the emerald in a strongbox, which he hid in a heavy steamer trunk in our room. He kept the keys to both on a chain around his neck. The only other keys to the strongbox were those held by his father, and another in a bank vault in Paris. The strongbox, made of wrought iron, was specially designed for moving the jewel, Mark told me. The craftsman boasted that it was impossible to break into — not an idle boast, either, because Mark asked me to try. So then we come to who stole the keys, I suppose."

Holmes glances with some interest and amusement at Watson. "A keen reasoner. We're fortunate, Watson, to have such an astute reporter."

You fight off a blush. "The keys were lost on the rugby field, according to Mark. He had just stolen the ball from Oxy after the scrum, and Oxy, apparently enraged, viciously tackled him and brought him to the ground. Mark had the wind knocked out of him and lay unconscious with Oxy on top of him, as everyone gathered round." *Check Clue RR*.

Holmes bends toward you. "Continue."

"When Mark came to, several minutes later, the keys and the chain were gone."

"And what of the other three boys — where were they?"

"All of us play rugby — it's compulsory — and we all gathered around him. Rafferty, who seldom leaves Oxy's side, even on the playing field, was close by. I cannot say about Bingley, although he is our star scrum-half and was on the field at the time."

"And Mueller?"

"Mr. Mueller, now that you mention him, is our rugby coach — he's an old Oxford rugger Blue. He played wing three-quarter for three Internationals, as he never tires of reminding us, when he was young, if he ever was young. He probably seemed fifty even then. Rugby gives him his big chance to make us run till we drop. I remember Mueller hurrying over to Mark and kneeling beside him to see if he was injured."

"So any one of them could have taken the chain from Mark," Mr. Holmes concludes.

You glance out the window at the crowd passing below. "I suppose. Or the chain could have fallen off, and perhaps someone found it later. I thought it was Oxy, because he was right on top of Mark, and he seemed so fascinated by the emerald. Oh, one other thing. This younger boy, Higby-Ross, told me he saw Bingley running towards the woods during the commotion that followed when Mueller cancelled practice." *Check Clue SS*.

"I see," says Holmes, lighting his pipe again. "When did Mark notice the strongbox was broken into?"

"When he got back from the infirmary, after dinner," you recall. "They took him to the infirmary because he was in such pain. But when he realized that the key might have been stolen instead of lost, he left the infirmary and hobbled over to our room. The strongbox was gone. Anyone could have stolen it during dinner. Of course the rooms were searched, but the thief could have hidden the jewel on the grounds or in the woods."

"So any of the five — the four students or the headmaster — could have stolen the key on the field, and taken the strongbox during dinner," Holmes concludes. *Check Clue TT*.

"Except that I was the only other one who knew where the strongbox was hidden," you remind Holmes. "That's why Mark accuses me. The strongbox was about the shape of a cigar box. Mark had a special false bottom in his steamer trunk and hid the box beneath that." *Check Clue YY*.

Again concern almost overwhelms you. "Since we were roommates and best friends, Mark showed the emerald to me — he was quite proud of his father's cleverness.

And he doesn't think anyone else could have discovered the box. Mr. Holmes, you must hurry! We're not getting anywhere toward solving the mystery!" In your frustration and fear, you rush to the window overlooking Baker Street.

"I am not certain that we have the proper clues to make any valid deductions," Holmes says, putting down his pipe. "But you have presented us with some points of singular interest. For example, how were the keys stolen in broad daylight before a crowd of boys? Who could have had enough access to your room to discover the false bottom to the trunk? And precisely where is the jewel? Also, is the Rafferty-boy the son of the well-known criminal, and if so, is he working for his father?" *Pick a number and add your Observation bonus:*
- *If 2-6, turn to 300.*
- *If 7-12, turn to 164.*

100

Becky Connoly and Richard Bingley enter the clearing. He takes from his pocket a billfold, and from the billfold some money. He gives a small wad of pound notes to Becky along with a piece of paper. You cannot hear him clearly but do make out something about "Paris... train... friend."

"....money..." she replies.

"Have you made the arrangements?"

You only hear her say: "Sir Richard." Then he hands her a gold ring. As they kiss, you decide you have seen enough and head back toward the school. *Check Clue V. Turn to 232.*

101

You cannot find the cave or locate Oxy and Muskrat. Discouraged, you decide to return to the school. *Turn to 159.*

102

You step aside as Lomax lunges at you and crashes against the car. He swells and puffs with anger, cursing into his mustache. He pushes off from the carriage door and lurches toward you. You try to slip beneath him, but his large hand grabs you, forcing you over the guard-rail that rings the platform. The landscape rushes past you upside down like white water over boulders, the tracks clacking above the roar of the wheels. Above you the ruffian's cheeks flush with anger as his hands tighten around your throat. You gasp for air and push against him, staggering with him back to the other side of the platform. The tracks beneath you slow as the train pulls into a station, the blur resolving into individual ralroad ties. The train's brakes squeal and hiss as you jump over the guardrail.

You tumble onto the ground, deflecting the impact of the fall, roadbed gravel stinging your hands. You stand, licking your palms where the skin is torn, as the train creaks into the station several hundred yards ahead. You set out after the train with a low, throbbing pain in your left knee. *Pick a number and add your Athletics bonus:*
- *If 2-6, turn to 295.*
- *If 7-12, turn to 146.*

103

You make your way warily into town. The road leads through the woods, but the bird calls you hear sound soothing and genuine.

You experience relief when you reach Main Street. After posting the letter to Holmes, you are handed a cable and a letter by the postmaster. The cable reads:

MUSKRAT FATHER PRIME CRIMINAL [STOP] MAY WELL HAVE HAND IN ROCK BUSINESS [STOP] CHECK POST AGAIN TOMORROW [STOP] BEST HOLMES [STOP]

Check Clue K.

The typed letter, with no return address, reads:

To a very smart boy:
Stay away, as you've been told. The cat, too, was curious. Mind your manners by minding your business, and you may become a gentleman.

As you walk down the post office steps, you notice a Clarence four-wheel carriage drive past with old man Rafferty and come to a stop at the intersection. Holmes's telegram crackles in your pocket.
• *If you try to grab on to the back of Rafferty's Clarence, turn to 137.*
• *Otherwise, turn to 250.*

104

The brief walk back into Belton Village clears your head. *Turn to 250.*

105

You enter the shop.
"Can I help you, lad?" a man gruffly asks, folding his arms. *Pick a number* and add your Artifice bonus:
• *If 2-6, turn to 153.*
• *If 7-12, turn to 194.*

106

You walk quickly toward Belton village from the school grounds, hoping to find a wire from Holmes at the Post Office. As you hurry down the drive, a carriage rattles past you. *Turn to 240.*

107

You approach the back wall, and reaching behind a tin of peas, you find a door handle. *Turn to 131.*

108

You stealthily move behind shelves, hiding, as the shopkeeper walks the aisles of the shop. Finally, he gives up, closes the lights, locks up the shop and leaves. Or is he just pretending to leave and setting a trap for you?
- *If you have checked Clue GG, turn to 131.*
- *Otherwise, turn to 325.*

109

You cannot decipher Miller's mumblings. The headmaster turns to the students, announcing: "Here, my young friends, is a lesson in dissolute living. Work hard, and you can achieve anything in the world. But lie about and play games, and you shall find yourself living in the gutter. Thank you, sir, for providing such a lesson to our students." Then Mueller gives Joe Miller a handshake and quickly ushers him off-stage. *Turn to 226.*

110

Rafferty sits behind a desk. A husky man with a bowler hat paces the floor, speaking very fast and softly to Rafferty.

"I tell you, mate, the whole business is off! Crowley is scared off. Won't touch it, mate," the man complains, upset.

"But we had a deal," Rafferty insists. "Fifteen thousand for the gem."

"He's scared off. Said he had no bargain for darts and savages and the like."

Rafferty snorts. "And he calls himself 'The Great Beast!' Have you tried any others?"

"I've tried Oatmeal, and George Quinby, and the Haggler. I've even brought the price down to ten thousand quid. No deal, mate. We haven't gotten the best publicity. Have you read the bloomin' clipping?"

He holds up a newspaper clipping.

"Scotland Yard, they are familiar with," the man asserts. "But not bleedin' Indians and magic and these bloomin' darts. They're spooked, mate. The Emerald is cursed!"

Rafferty waves his hand impatiently. "Superstition."

"And was it superstition that got Mahoney? No thank you, mate. You take the treasure and welcome to it."

"Don't be such a bloody fool. They got Mahoney because he's a drunk and a fool," says Rafferty, pointing a scrawny finger. "And a braggart. They have no way of discovering we have the jewel."

"They got to the school, didn't they?" he argues. "Didn't your lad say his mates were telling tales of savages in the woods... They're mystic-like, and deadly, those little fellows."

"Well, fifteen thousand pounds isn't mystic-like," Rafferty snaps. "And one of the prettiest jewels that you will ever see."

"But I haven't seen it. Where is the jewel?" The man's eyes gleam with greed.

"Trust, my friend. Our business is based on trust. Get busy and find a buyer. Try any foreign agents. Try the Welshman. The Welshman might be interested. Ten percent for anyone who can find a buyer."

"You're whistlin' in the dark, mate, barkin' at the moon."

"You will soon be out in the cold, whistling and barking," says Rafferty as he stands.

You crouch, poised to leave. *Check Clue L. Turn to 111.*

111

You push against the wall, and the wall turns. You slip through to the grocer's shop. Glowering, Lomax stands above you. "Going somewhere?" *Pick a number and add your Athletics bonus:*
- *If 2-6, turn to 147.*
- *If 7-12, turn to 259.*

112

An empty tin lies on the floor nearby. You edge over to it and turn yourself so that the tin is behind you. Then you pick it up with your left hand, and using the sharp edge of the lid, cut the ropes. Free, you frantically search the room for clues, but to no avail. Through a door you emerge into the greengrocer's shop, which is closed and dark. You steal out of the shop and run as fast as your feet will fly.
- *If you return to 221B Baker Street, turn to 341.*
- *If you return to Belton School, turn to 218.*

113

"Mr. Mueller stole the Emerald!" you cry. *Turn to 365.*

114

Oxy runs from the cave, and peering down, discovers you. "So, he likes punishment, does he?" Oxy snarls, pulling you into the cave. *Turn to 154.*

115

You reach the following deductions: whoever made the bootprints (A) followed whoever made the shoeprints (B) along the cart-road. (B) entered the clearing and sat on the log, waiting for (C). (A) hid behind the trees for a while, as you can tell by the way his bootprints broaden into a wider, circular area. He waited and watched as the owner of the female bootprints (C) entered the clearing, an ideal spot for a tryst, where she was met by (B), and they embraced. From the presence of the rose, you deduce she was his girlfriend; the seclusion indicates they were having a romantic rendezvous. (A) crept behind the trees to watch. Enraged, he ran into the circle and accosted (B), giving the signs of a scuffle, and was hurled to the mud. He returned, disconsolate, to school; (B) and (C) left together for town, where (C) probably lives. *Check Clue VV. Turn to 311.*

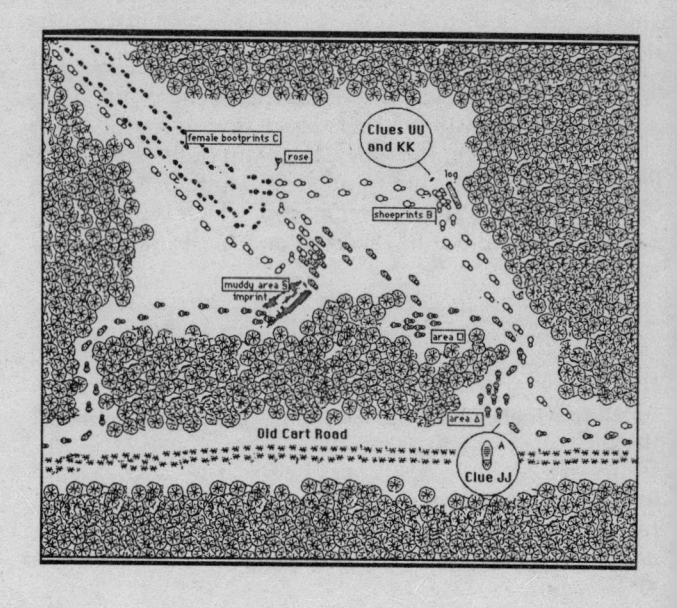

116

You overhear Oxy threaten Muskrat about the money that Muskrat owes him from gambling — and losing. "I'll collect somehow."

Muskrat Rafferty whines: "I, I'll get the money before the holidays."

"For your sake, friend, you'd better!" Oxy snaps. "But where will you get it?"

"I have a certain item of value I'm negotiating the sale of," Rafferty mysteriously replies.

Oxfield says that if Muskrat doesn't get the money, he will take the item itself plus collect the interest in pain. He gives Rafferty until the Christmas holiday break. The boys part as Oxy shoves Muskrat away. *Check Clue O. Turn to 290.*

117

You slip into the cave without being noticed and hide among Muskrat's stolen treasure, ducking behind an old trunk used for shipping clothing. *Turn to 351.*

118

The comings and goings of the various sets of footprints leave you befuddled. Too confused to sort them out, you decide to return to Belton School. *Turn to 311.*

119

Lomax slugs you, and you fall, hitting the ground hard, the landscape spinning around you like a calliope whirling out of control. You lie on the ground, trying to stop the sky from tumbling over you and the ground beneath from spinning. Your arm aches and you have a sharp pain in your thigh. *Reduce your Athletics bonus by 1 for the remainder of this adventure.* You slowly stand. **Pick a number** *and add your Athletics bonus:*
- *If 2-8, turn to 295.*
- *If 9-12, turn to 146.*

11

120

You sneak closer to the glass. Bingley hands the pawnbroker three items: a watch, a tie clasp, and a small jewel box. The owner opens the box, and purses his lips, whistling. You strain to catch a better glimpse of what the box holds, but the item is turned away from you. *Turn to 317.*

121

You leave the office, return to your room, and slip into bed, praying for a peaceful, swift conclusion to the mystery. *Turn to 206.*

122

You knock on the door, and hearing no reply, slip into Oxy's room. You check his desk and suitcases but find nothing of interest. Then, hidden under nightshirts in his top bureau drawer is a box which shimmers when you open it. A trove of jewels, marbles, polished stones, shells, even a chunk of mica rest inside the box. *Check Clue WW*. You try to tell if the jewels are real. *Pick a number and add your Scholarship bonus:*
- *If 2-7, turn to 136.*
- *If 8-12, turn to 221.*

123

Becky sighs. "No, Mark. I know what you're thinking. Shame! Richard told me about the jewel. I was sorry to hear about it. But he did not steal it. And I think you know he didn't."

Mark picks up a rock from the ground and flings it toward a tree. "Perhaps not, but he stole the one valuable I really care about — you. Well, I must go. They'll miss me at Latin." *Check Clue CC*. Mark walks off in silence.

You watch as Becky sits on the rim of a stone fountain and begins to weep. Suddenly, she runs into the house, and ten minutes later, emerges with a suitcase. Intrigued, you follow her to the Belton train station.
- *If you follow her on the train, turn to 307.*
- *Otherwise, turn to 218.*

124

You turn the knob, but the safe will not open. *Pick a number and add your Artifice bonus:*
- *If 2-11, turn to 121.*
- *If 12, turn to 228.*

125

Rafferty and the man in the bowler hat come into the room. Rafferty bends down to hiss in your face.

"So we have a sneaky little ferret on our trail."

Rafferty stands and kicks you hard in the ribs. Pain takes your breath away.

Then he removes the gag. "Just a sample, lad, a very mild sample of what is to come. Now tell me: why have you been sneaking around here?" The man in the bowler hat shakes his fist in your face.

"You can save yourself some pain..." Rafferty says, ominously.

"I...am trying to recover the jewel," you say.

"Everyone's so greedy. Even schoolboys. How discouraging," Rafferty says.

"I don't want it for myself," you explain. "It's for Mark. His father's in danger — from the Indians."

"Friendship. How touching," Mr. Rafferty sneers.

"What was I telling you?" the man in the bowler hat practically whispers. "Those bloomin' Indians. They're mystic, like. It's like they're everywhere."

Rafferty sneers. "Ridiculous."

Suddenly a dart whizzes by and sticks into the wall with a loud "thwock!" The man with the bowler hat cries out "Savages!" and pushes the wall open. He and Rafferty rush off through the shop, knocking tins from their shelves. Then a Black River Indian emerges from the window and chases after them.

You struggle against the ropes that bind you. An empty tin lies on the floor nearby. You edge over to it and turn yourself so that the tin is behind you. You pick it up the can with your left hand, and using the sharp edge of the lid, cut the ropes.

Free, you hurry after the others, but they have disappeared.

- *If you go to 221B Baker Street, turn to 341.*
- *Otherwise, turn to 126.*

126

You decide to take the train back to Belton School, wondering how you will explain your absence. *Turn to 218.*

127

You gaze at the cigar butt. *Pick a number and add your Scholarship bonus:*
- *If 2-7, turn to 217*
- *If 8-12, turn to 248.*

128

You notice Rafferty approach the back wall, which has shelves of canned goods. He reaches behind a tin of Braxton's Peas, gives a push, and the wall revolves. Rafferty slips into a back room, and the wall returns to its normal position, a tin of peas tipping over as the wall door closes. *Check Clue GG.*
- *If you enter the shop, turn to 105.*
- *If you return to 221B Baker Street, turn to 297.*

129

Mueller had knelt beside the fallen boy while all of the other players gathered around Mark on the ground. Mr. Mueller brushed them aside and held Mark's head in his hands, testing Mark's awareness and reflexes with a curious circular motion of his hands in front of Mark's face. He was the only other suspect who spent much time near Mark when he was knocked out. *Check Clue B.* Of course, the chain and key could simply have come off, fallen onto the grass and been found by any of the supects. *Turn to 361.*

130

After classes the next day, you walk through the woods to the village, to send your letter and wire to Holmes. As you make your way through the woods, you notice Muskrat walking ahead of you. He appears to be slinking toward the cliffs, where the caves are.
- *If you follow him, turn to 243.*
- *Otherwise, turn to 195.*

131

You turn the handle hidden behind the tins of peas and push. The wall panel turns. You slip into the back room and hide behind stacked cider barrels. ***Pick a number and add your Artifice bonus:***
- *If 2-6, turn to 111.*
- *If 7-12, turn to 110.*

132

You study the dart, which has a sharp metal point like that of a fishhook, and holds a black liquid at the tip: curare? You carefully wrap the dart in your handkerchief before walking toward the village. ***Turn to 265.***

133

You dash down the steps and out the door, ignoring Dr. Watson's cries to stop. As you reach the street, you see Muskrat turn off into another street and give chase. You reach the corner and see him step past an old lady with a parasol in the heart of a crowd. You push on, struggling to reach him. ***Pick a number*** *and add your Athletics Bonus:*
- *If 2-7, turn to 338.*
- *If 8-12, turn to 279.*

134

"He's after me!" you cry.

"After you? Who's that, lad?" the train attendant asks with a doubtful smile.

Lomax barges through the railway car doors.

"He is! That man!"

The attendant laughs, his florid cheeks puffing out. "Don't be absurd, lad. Now be a good boy and take your seat."

"But that man is out to — "

"Take your seat, lad. You've had your fun," the attendant says, clearly not believing you. "We shall be pulling into the station soon."

You dash off down the aisle, Lomax lumbering after you.

You exit onto the platform and step to the next one. You try to get into the next car, but the door will not open. The platform shifts uneasily beneath you as the tracks rush past further below. You tug on the door but a hand slams against it above yours. You jump back to the opposite platform, and the ruffian with the black brows lunges toward you. *Pick a number and add your Athletics bonus:*
- *If 2-6, turn to 119.*
- *If 7-12, turn to 102.*

135

That evening at dinner, Master Mueller announces that Richard Bingley's cufflinks, watch and tie-clasp have been stolen. He asks the thief to step forward immediately, but no one stirs. *Check Clue F.* As punishment, dessert is not served.

Later that night, as you are supposed to be studying, you contemplate Oxy as the possible thief. Oxy straddled Mark on the playing field as Mark lay unconscious, and with his strength he could have ripped the chain from him. In many ways, Oxy seems the most likely suspect. Both he and Muskrat are failing several subjects and must attend a compulsory evening study session at Perkins Hall; their room is now empty.
- *If you search Oxy's room, turn to 122.*
- *Otherwise, turn to 204.*

136
You study the jewels, but cannot determine their value. *Turn to 236.*

137
You run up to the carriage. ***Pick a number** and add your Athletics bonus:*
- *If 2-7, turn to 148.*
- *If 8-12, turn to 267.*

138
Wary of the Indians, you follow Bingley through the woods to town. He strolls down Main Street to Elm Street. *Turn to 200.*

139
A cigar band with the letters "Galliardi" lies nearby. ***Pick a number** and add your Observation bonus:*
- *If 2-8, turn to 217.*
- *if 9-12, turn to 249.*

140
You cannot hear them clearly. Sir Richard sounds very angry.

"Have you considered what this will do to your mother?" he thunders. His son says something inaudible. "And to our social standing? What do you know about this girl?" his father presses. "This, this trollop! This will break your mother's heart."

Richard's reply cannot be heard.

"And how will you support her?"

You hear only: " — all she needs. — sufficient funds."

"What funds?"

" — assets I can sell."

"Well, you will get no help from me," concludes Sir Richard.

" — your help."

"I forbid you to marry her!" says Sir Richard.

You hear footsteps coming down the hall and must hide. *Check Clue S. Turn to 285.*

141

A sharp cracking sound comes from behind you; the branch is breaking! ***Pick a number and add your Athletics bonus:***
- *If 2-7, turn to 314.*
- *If 8-12, turn to 220.*

142

Later, in geometry class, you check your notebook.
- *If you have checked Clue N, turn to 304.*
- *Otherwise, turn to 189.*

143

You follow the bootprints up the cart-road. Weeds and tall grasses jut between the parallel tracks of the road. A slender tree leans across the road like a gate in the distance. You notice a different set of shoeprints along the road as well. ***Pick a number and add your Observation bonus:***
- *If 2-4, turn to 144.*
- *If 5-12, turn to 230.*

OLD CART ROAD

144

The prints follow the cart-path for a quarter-mile, and then you lose them. Looking to one side, you spy them heading into the woods and follow.

The shoeprints go directly into the clearing and lead to a log beside the trees, where they obscure each other with their profusion. ***Pick a number and add your Observation bonus:***
- *If 2-7, turn to 217.*
- *If 8-12, turn to 302.*

145

Bingley comes toward you, and stands hands on hips, looking for you. Becky calls him back from the gate. Perhaps loath to waste their time together, he turns and joins her in the garden. Relieved, you hobble off through the woods back to school. ***Turn to 223.***

146

You slowly trot toward the train ahead of you, your limbs aching, hoping to climb aboard at the station. As you come up to the station, the train sits stalled amidst a commotion beside the baggage car steps. A tall foreigner in flamboyant dress, surrounded by a crowd of onlookers, stands gesticulating at the train attendant. Heavy bands of astrakhan across the foreigner's sleeves seem to slash the air, while the deep blue cloak which is thrown over his shoulders flares with a flame-colored silk lining at each of his overwrought gestures.

"My baggage sir! I must have my baggage!" the gentleman insists.

"Sir, we have shown you the only steamer trunk that the baggage car contains! You must have left your baggage at your station of origin," insists the porter.

"I, sir, left my baggage! No, sir! Do you think I am in the habit of carrying my own baggage, and associating with porters!?"

"Sir, I had no intention of implying.." the attendant stammers.

"Do you know who I am? I am Wilhelm Gottsriech Sigismond von Ormstein, Grand Duke of Cassel-Felstein and ..."

You quietly slip up the steps and onto the train, taking your seat in the back of the car. *Turn to 244.*

147

A huge fist the size of a ham flies toward you and knocks you out. *Turn to 173.*

148

You grab the rail running around the top of the carriage (where the luggage rests) and settle onto the axle below just as the carriage takes off. The rattling ride takes you toward the train station. With no warning, a trunk shifts and crushes your fingers against the rail. The carriage dips and jumps, and you tumble to the ground, stunned and out of breath. The carriage pulls away, and rubbing your injured hand, you decide to return to school. *Turn to 250.*

149

Something in your manner makes Miller suspicious, and after trying and failing to grab the shilling, he stumbles off down the street, cursing under his breath. *Turn to 283.*

150

However pleasant, the waterfall leads you nowhere. As you walk back toward the school, you come on a seldom-used path leading away from campus. *Pick a number and add your Intuition bonus:*
- *If 2-9, turn to 273.*
- *If 10-12, turn to 175.*

151

From your position, you cannot discern what they are saying.
- *If you try to slip into the cave, turn to 346.*
- *Otherwise, turn to 342.*

152

You ask for permission to leave the table and follow the father and son at a distance. They enter a classroom and close the door. *Pick a number and add your Artifice bonus:*
- *If 2-7, turn to 165.*
- *If 8-12, turn to 140.*

153

You move down the aisle. "I'm closing up, lad. So let's be brisk."

A customer enters the store. You slip behind the far set of shelves. The customer buys tins of meat and leaves. "Lad? Lad?" The grocer mutters to himself and comes looking for you.

- *If you stay hidden in the store, pick a number and add your Artifice bonus:*
  - *If 2-7, turn to 333.*
  - *If 8-12, turn to 108.*
- *If you leave the store and return to 221B Baker Street, turn to 297.*

154

Oxy raises a fist to knock you silly. *Pick a number and add your Athletics bonus:*
- *If 2-7, turn to 169.*
- *If 8-12, turn to 288.*

155

Something about their manner bothers you; you decide to follow Oxy from dinner. *Pick a number and add your Artifice bonus:*
- *If 2-8, turn to 210.*
- *If 9-12, turn to 275.*

156

The letter is almost impossible to decipher. *Pick a number and add your Intuition bonus:*
- *If 2-7, turn to 255.*
- *If 8-12, turn to 335.*

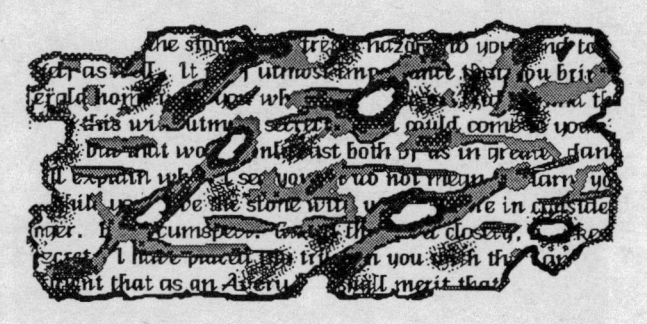

157

Something pierces your arm; the sky swims above as you pass out. When you come to, your muscles ache and you burn with a fever. *Pick a number and add your Athletics bonus:*
- *If 2-5, turn to 343.*
- *If 6-12, turn to 370.*

158

Though their voices are low, you can hear them. "Oh, Richard! How could you afford this? I thought your father didn't approve," coos Becky, delighted.

"I sold some things I didn't need."

"Richard, I don't need all these presents." She embraces him again. "I have you."

"I like giving pretty things to you."

As they embrace, you notice a pendant with a stone hanging from a chain around her neck. *Check Clue N.* You creep forward on the branch to see and hear better. *Pick a number and add your Artifice bonus:*
- *If 2-10, turn to 141.*
- *If 11-12, turn to 320.*

159

As you make your way through the woods, you see Mark ahead of you, obviously taking the back way into town.
- *If you follow him, turn to 201.*
- *Otherwise, turn to 106.*

160

You run to the administration building. Struggling to lift yourself on to the window ledge, you peer through a crack in the curtains. Rafferty stands beside Mueller's desk. Losing your balance, you fall against the window and drop back to the ground. Afraid you've been noticed, you run down the drive and past the main gate. ***Turn to 229.***

161

That night, after lights out, you sneak over to Master Mueller's office and attempt to unlock the door with your knife. ***Pick a number and add your Artifice bonus:***
- *If 2-6, turn to 354.*
- *If 7-12, turn to 168.*

162

The carriage slowly pulls up beside you. A man jumps from the carriage onto the fruit cart. You struggle with him as the streets whirl past, and stunned pedestrians watch. *Pick a number and add your Athletics bonus:*
- *If 2-7, turn to 147.*
- *If 8-12, turn to 260.*

163

From your Latin studies, you understand 'Caveat emptor" to mean "Let the buyer beware."

"My favorite writings from the classics," you reply, "are in Greek. Socrates is quite apt with 'Knote autein', for example." From your Greek studies you understand 'Knote autein' to mean 'Know thyself'.

Mueller smiles darkly. "You exceed me there. Look to our native writers. As the Bard has it: 'It is the bright day that brings forth the adder, and thus craves wary walking.' "

"I like the passage: 'I come not to praise Ceasar but to bury him.' "

"I have no doubt that is a favorite passage with students," Miller replies, seething. "Mine has always been:

*"And Caesar's spirit, ranging for revenge,
Shall in these confines with a monarch's voice,
Cry 'Havoc!' and let slip the dogs of war...'"*

You smile. "Yes, many of us guessed you would enjoy that. Mr. Miller seems to enjoy Iago's 'Put money in thy pocket.'"

Mueller frowns. "I find Polonius's 'neither a borrower nor a lender be', even more helpful," he adds.

You smile. "Seems a bit cold to me. Especially when you've got someone like Joe Miller in need. All men are brothers, we are told."

Mr. Mueller glares at you. "And we have a proverb about curiosity and a cat." *Check Clue ZZ.*

"Well," you say, "this conversation, like Mr. Miller's, was most instructive. But that is what education is all about." Rising, you join the other students by the biscuit trays. For the remainder of the tea, you catch the headmaster giving you sidelong glances. Perhaps Joe Miller was telling the truth. *Check Clue G. Turn to 135.*

164

As if summoned up by mentioning him, you notice Muskrat Rafferty making his way along the street below Holmes' window.

"That's him!" You bend toward the window, astonished to see Rafferty strolling down Baker Street.
- *If you follow him, turn to 133.*
- *If you stay with Mr. Holmes and Dr. Watson, turn to 300.*

165

You cannot hear them clearly. Sir Richard sounds very angry.

" — your mother?"

Young Richard says something in a soft voice.

" — break your mother's heart."

They speak softly, and you cannot understand them.

Sir Richard walks to the door. "Well, son, you will get no help from me."

" — your help," says your schoolmate.

You hear footsteps coming down the hall and hide. ***Turn to 285.***

166

The sign reads:

> YOU OWE ME. FRIDAY.
> STICKS AND STONES
> WILL BREAK YOUR BONES.

Check Clue W. Turn to 364.

167

You hunker down in the seat and turn toward the window, disguising your face as a mask of idiocy. The scenery rushes by as a shadow crosses your lap. Lomax moves past and returns to his seat without noticing you. *Turn to 244.*

168

With a loud click, the lock gives and you enter Mueller's office like a criminal and search around. The headmaster's desk lamp is conveniently lighted. Behind the painting on the wall, you find a safe. Searching in the desk drawers, you find several letters. The top letter, typed, reads:

Dear Sir:

We have been honored and privileged to provide your school with textbooks for eight years. We sincerely hope that we may provide these materials in the future. We are pleased to extend credit to such a worthy institution.

However, as we have received no payment for the last six months, and as the debt is beyond our means to continue to extend, we must hereby cut off all credit, and call for the payment of the outstanding balance.

We trust in your good faith.

> *Sincerely yours,*
> *Messrs. Pomroy & Ross*
> *Savoy Publications, Ltd.*

Check Clue Z. The other letters — from suppliers of coal, food, etc. — have an angrier tone. You roughly estimate the school debt to be over 5,000 pounds. Then you come upon a series of letters from the Northern Bank of Edinburgh.

Dear Sir:

As we indicated to you at the time, land investments in the Western United States are an extremely speculative form of investment. Differing claims from various states, treaties with Indian tribes, conflicting claims of settlers, as well as a variety of other factors such as changing laws regarding taxing of land holdings, railroad routes, etc., make this particular form of an investment extremely speculative. Fortunes have beeen made and lost in these matters.

Unfortunately, your investments in the Montana Land Co. have been of the latter sort. The Montana Land Co. has since been declared bankrupt, returning only 1/10th (one tenth) of the investment value to the investors. We hereby enclose a cheque for eighty pounds.

If we may be of service to you in the future, please feel free to contact us.

> *Yours,*
>
> *Harold Montague*
>
> *Harold Montague, Agent*
> *Northern Bank of Edinburgh.*

Other letters reveal a series of investment losses over eight years totaling roughly 4,346 pounds. *Check Clue P.*

Suddenly, you hear a noise from outside the office and dim the lamp. Footsteps come to the door. *Pick a number and add your Artifice bonus:*
- *If 2-4, turn to 336.*
- *If 5-8, turn to 298.*
- *If 9-12, turn to 270.*

169

Like a bull stung by a bee, Oxy snorts with rage and rushes at you. You crash against the trunk and wriggle free of the oaf's grasp. Then Muskrat reaches down among the silverware and picking up a fork, comes toward you. You reach down and pick up a silver tea-service tray and a ladle. The fork clangs against the tray and bounces off. You parry Muskrat's thrusts with your ladle, as Oxy picks up a porcelain teapot and sends the white globe flying toward you. Before you can dodge it, the teapot strikes you in the chest and knocks you back. As you recover, Muskrat and Oxy charge you. Shifting your balance, you duck, and Oxy crashes into Muskrat with an "Oof!" Cursing, they hit the ground together.

"You bleeding idiot!" Muskrat whines, trying to get to his feet.

"Shut your mouth, or I'll — " thunders Oxy.

"Clumsy hulk!"

You stand up, aching, and hobble from the cave, trying to escape the fallen pair.

"Fool!" Oxy cries.

"Where did he go?"

"He got away..."

You stumble toward the woods and hide in some dense shrubbery until they give up looking for you and leave. *Turn to 159.*

170

The blotting paper retains a reverse image of what was written, so that if you hold the paper up to a mirror or glass, you may be able to read the writing. You do so, using the glass case holding Mueller's rugby trophies and read:

> Joe.
>
> I told you that I can no longer help you.
> You must leave this area. I will not
> submit to your blackmail. Do not count
> my promise to mother.
>
> Karl

Pick a number and add your Intuition bonus:
- *If 2-5, turn to 330.*
- *If 6-12, turn to 171.*

171

The note reads:

> *Joe:*
>
> *I told you I can no longer help you.
> You must leave this area. I will not
> submit to your blackmail. Do not rely
> upon my promise to mother.*
>
> *Karl.*

Check Clue Q. Turn to 330.

172

You bring your heel down hard on Lomax's toe. He lets out a groan, and you run down the drive and past the main gate. The ox lopes after you awhile, then gives up and turns back to Perkins Hall. ***Turn to 229.***

173

When you regain consciousness, you are bound and gagged in a darkened room. You struggle against the ropes that bind you. ***Pick a number and add your Artifice bonus:***
- *If 2-7, turn to 125.*
- *If 8-12, turn to 112.*

174

That night you have a dream. You are climbing a tree in the forest, a tree choked with vines. As you climb, the vines seem to wrap around you and bind you. Struggling, you reach a high branch. Below you, Becky Connoly, even more beautiful than before, climbs toward you, reaching out. The touch of her skin on yours sends a thrill over you like a drop of oil spreading over water. The Black River Emerald dangles from a chain around her neck. As she climbs onto the branch with you, it bends and breaks beneath you. You tumble toward the ground and awaken in a cold sweat. *Turn to 292.*

175

The path cuts through tall ferns and shrubs, ending near a boulder and the partially-hidden mouth of a cave. *Turn to 281.*

176

You walk back to the grocer's shop. As you're standing across the street, watching the shop windows, you are violently seized from behind and knocked out. *Turn to 173.*

177

What next, you wonder.
- *If you want to search the cave that you saw Muskrat heading toward yesterday, turn to 263.*
- *Otherwise, turn to 142.*

178

You slip into the cave and to your horror, find a fist grabbing your shirt.

"So, he likes punishment, does he?" Oxy snarls, shaking you. *Turn to 154.*

179

Pain trickles down your arm from Oxy's blow, and your arm goes limp. *Reduce your Athletics bonus by 1 for the remainder of this adventure.* Oxy smiles, and draws his fist back again. "Going through my things, eh?" He twists your arm, grabbing you from behind in a full Nelson. "Muskrat, be my guest." Muskrat glows with pleasure.

Rafferty comes toward you, and you lift up and kick him back with your feet. He tumbles back and hits the wall. "Want to play?" Oxy says, punching you from behind. He pushes you and butts your head repeatedly into the wall. Muskrat grabs a shovel from the fireplace implements and swings it at you. *Pick a number and add your Athletics bonus:*
- *If 2-7, turn to 358.*
- *If 8-12, turn to 280.*

The return address is 221B Baker Street. You tear at the envelope, and read:

Mr. David Rogers   *December 18*
Belton School
Belton Village

Dear David:

The matter you mentioned to me has taken on considerable importance. Were I not involved in matters concerning some of the highest statesmen in Europe, and the threat of war, I should come myself. You and your friend are in grave peril. The Black River Emerald is the sacred treasure of a South American Indian tribe who live along the Black River, a tributary of the mighty Amazon. The Black River Indians, a particularly fierce warrior tribe, regard the emerald as their sacred talisman, from which they derive the power to conquer hostile neighboring tribes. They believe that the emerald is a star in the constellation of Orion, whom they call Guerro, the warrior god. The star fell to earth during a fierce battle with enemy gods, and turned the color of the jungle. At any rate, without this stone, the Black River Indians are powerless; their warriors will attempt to recover the stone at any cost.

The Black River Indians were visited by Irish missionaries earlier in this century, who brought back tales of a fabulous green gem to our shores. A certain unscrupulous Irish trader named Mahoney got wind of the stone and ventured to South America in search of that and other treasure. I have dealt with him before and he is of the crudest sort. He smells of greed. Having seen what drink has done to so many of his countrymen, he employs its awesome powers in his own interests, to rob the gullible. And who better than a tribe of primitives, unfamiliar with the dizzying juice of the vine and the juniper berry? Having befriended the chieftains of the tribe, he plied them with liquor for days, and walked away with their treasure while the Indians laughed or slept. He brought the stone here and sold it to Sir Winston Avery, a wealthy collector of gems and art.

When the Indians regained their senses, having exhausted the store of gin he left them, they found their heads weak, their stomachs queasy, and their treasure gone. To those with as keen a nose and as fine a tracking skill as the Black River Indians, tracing Mahoney's foul scent was easy. Perhaps he thought they wouldn't dare cross a great ocean. Perhaps he underestimated their devotion to the stone. Whatever the case, he has paid dearly. I enclose a newspaper clipping to which I direct your attention.

The best guess is that two or three of the Indians have come to our shores as stow-aways to find the stone. They probably acquired a smattering of English from the missionaries, so they are not entirely lost here.

If they could trace the stone to Mahoney, they can trace the stone to Sir Avery, and to Belton School. You must find the emerald, and give it to Mark, so that he can return it to the Indians, for the stone belongs to them. Whoever is so greedy as to grasp this "star that burns" will meet Mahoney's fate. If the warriors catch up to Mark, and find that he can't give them the stone, he may forfeit his life. Contact the village constabulary. They can at least provide you and your friend with a measure of safety. Surely Sir Avery would prefer his son alive to any treasure. Wire me as soon as you have any trace of the jewel. If possible, I will come to Belton very soon.

Yours in haste,
Sherlock Holmes.

P.S. A useful note: the Black River Indians call to each other using a distinctive bird-like cry. P.P.S. I will send a telegram tomorrow regarding Mr. Rafferty. Come to the Post Office to pick it up, to avoid arousing interest.

You read the enclosed newspaper clipping.

Art Dealer Found Paralyzed

Found paralyzed in his rooms yesterday was the Irish art dealer Timothy Mahoney. In a bizarre and puzzling incident, Mr. Mahoney was found with a dart in his neck. The dart was tipped with poison, according to Inspector Lestrade of Scotland Yard. Mr. Mahoney was unable to move or speak, and has not recovered.

Mahoney has had a somewhat dubious reputation in the art business. An adventurer and fortune hunter, he has travelled to distant regions of the world in pursuit of treasure. According to Inspector Lestrade, Scotland Yard has several valuable leads and continues to investigate the bizarre attack.

After reading the article, you wonder if you should go to the village constable with the dart and Holmes' letter, but you remember Mark's desire to keep the theft a secret. You decide to return to school to show him the letter and the dart. Warily you make your way back to the school via the main road, a mile and a half long journey. At an old cart-road leading off through the woods, you notice bootprints. *Pick a number and add your Observation bonus:*
- *If 2-5, turn to 245.*
- *If 6-12, turn to 326.*

181

You return to Belton and your usual schedule. *Turn to 142.*

182

You run through the woods, toward where you believe the cave to be, and spy Muskrat and Oxy hurrying ahead of you. *Turn to 289.*

183

The drunkard's breath washes over you.

"Who is this famous brother of yours?" you inquire.

Miller lunges for the shilling. *Pick a number and add your Artifice bonus:*
- *If 2-7, turn to 359.*
- *If 8-12, turn to 355.*

184

You race through the woods, the odd bird cries behind you; they abate as you reach the clearing behind your dormitory. You run up the steps to your dormitory, sighing with relief. *Turn to 142.*

185

You return to your dormitory to find Mark before going to 221B Baker Street. As you walk to your room, a man with a grizzled beard comes out of the rooms of Mr. Quigley, the Classics Instructor.

"She's missing, sir! Gone!" the man cries. "And it was with one of your boys—one of your fine, nice-mannered boys, I'm certain. One of your fine, high-toned lads come and stole her. My daughter was all I lived for. And he stole her away, to treat her for his pleasure, most-like."

You decide to go to Richard Bingley's room. Inside, an envelope addressed to Sir Richard Bingley, the boy's father, lies on the desk. You decide to take the envelope to Mr. Quigley, who thanks you, and return to your room. *Check Clue FF.*

As you enter your room, you are grabbed from behind.

A spear is pointed at your throat; you get the message and silence the scream rising from within. Two Indians stand beside Mark, their faces dark with paint, black lines zig-zagging down their torsoes, brandishing their spears at him. His wide eyes display terror.

"They want the Emerald!" Mark cries. "If you know who took it, for God's sake, tell them!"

You must solve the mystery now, to save Mark and yourself.

- If you accuse Oxy Oxfield, turn to 253.
- If you accuse Richard Bingley, turn to 321.
- If you accuse Headmaster Mueller, turn to 113.
- If you accuse Muskrat Rafferty, turn to 324.
- If you don't know what to do, turn to 365.

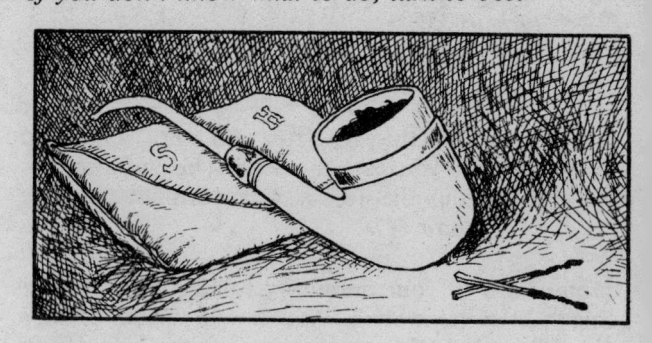

186

You interpret the letter further:

...the stone.. (ex)tre(me)... hazard to you and to (my)self as well..........................you bring (em)erald home... you wh(en you come).....
this with utm(ost)... secrecy... (I) could come .. you ...that wo(uld).. (o)nl(y). (c)ast both.. in great dan(ger) hil yo(u) (ha)ve the stone wit(h)... e in consider(able).. (da)nger. B(e) circumspect...closely.
(s)ecret I have tr n you h th. and
nt that as an Avery (you) shall merit that...
Turn to 255.

187

You race after the bird cries and catch up to them. Then a dart strikes the tree in front of you. *Pick a number and add your Artifice bonus:*
- *If 2-8, turn to 254.*
- *If 9-12, turn to 184.*

188

When you regain consciousness, Mark has left. The room is chilly and dark, the fire fading. You slowly stand, and almost black out again as you lean over to pick up the crumpled sheet beside the glowing embers in the fireplace. You slump into a chair, smooth out the darkened sheet on the desk, and prepare to read the letter, hoping Mark will forgive you. *Turn to 156.*

189

Nothing clarifies in your head; it's all such a muddle that even plane geometry seems simple in comparison. *Turn to 232.*

190

At the window, you purchase a second class ticket to London for two shillings. *Deduct the expense from your Money on your Character Record.* Boarding the train, you walk through the cars till you spy Rafferty and Lomax sitting together. You take a seat several rows behind them.

The train pulls out and picks up speed. Suddenly Lomax stands and walks toward you, his eyes meeting yours. *Pick a number and add your Artifice bonus:*
- *If 2-7, turn to 256.*
- *If 8-12, turn to 167.*

191

You conjure up a boot lying sideways beneath a bed, Mark's bed. The prints are from Mark's boots, recently bought at Harris's boot-shop in the Strand. *Check Clue JJ.*
- *If you follow the bootprints, turn to 143.*
- *Otherwise, turn to 311.*

192

You overhear Oxy gruffly whisper to Muskrat, "At the Pillars. At eight."

At fifteen minutes to eight, you walk to the Pillars, a set of columns behind the administration building, and hide behind a pillar. From the shadows, Oxy and Muskrat appear. *Turn to 116.*

193

From the portico of Perkins Hall, you notice Mark slip into the woods, heading toward town.
- *If you follow him, turn to 201.*
- *Otherwise, turn to 106.*

194

"I have some merchandise for you," you say shyly.

"What can you mean? A lad like you? What merchandise?" The man looks like he might threaten you.

"Freshest fruit you can lay your hands on," you say. "Selling them for me dad. He took sick and asked me to get any price I could. Out in the cart, they are, just up the street. Name me a price."

"Well, I'll go have a once-over," the man replies. He leaves the store and walks up the street to the fruit cart.
- *If you return to 221B Baker Street, turn to 297.*
- *If you search for the secret door, turn to 107.*

195

You hear the plaintive cries of birds in the trees. As you make your way toward the village, the bird cries intensify on either side of you. You look up in the trees and the sun's rays, piercing the forest gloom, blind you. Where are the birds? A sharp knock sounds against the tree beside you as a dart sticks into the trunk. What in the world!? You turn and see a small, painted figure running behind the trees to your left, as bird-cries echo through the forest. Indians in England!?
- *If you chase the figure, turn to 272.*
- *If you examine the dart, turn to 294.*
- *If you continue toward the village, turn to 357.*

196

You must decide what to do next.
- *If you follow Oxy, turn to 155.*
- *Otherwise, turn to to 290.*

197

"M'boy!" Watson greets you at the door. "My heavens, but you're a bit worse for wear. Come in, come in, and rest yourself! I'm afraid I must be off, though. Message from Holmes—he's on the scent again. How is the emerald affair resting? No, please, don't move. You must stay here tonight and rest. You look positively haggard. Holmes has gone off and won't be home at least till tomorrow night, if I read this right. You may use the couch. Slept there a number of times myself — much better than an Afghan mountainside, eh? Ring for Mrs. Hudson, and order some brothor whatever you like. Must run." And he dashes off.

Mrs. Hudson cooks you a fine meal of steak and potatoes, and gives you fresh sheets and towels. The next day, you must decide what to do.
- *If you return to the grocery, turn to 176.*
- *If you return to Belton School, turn to 218.*

198

You turn the corner and notice Bingley entering a shop. He buys a ribbon and a decorated box. Leaving the shop, he walks down sides streets of the town at a dizzying clip.
- *If you follow him, turn to 200.*
- *Otherwise, turn to 223.*

You try to slip the note beneath the book, but Mark's hand comes down on yours. He crumples the paper in his hand.

"Going through my things, too?" he says, enraged.

"Mark," you cry, "I'm your friend. I'm trying to help you. You're in great danger! The Indians who owned the jewel have come to reclaim it — that is why your father wants you to return it to him. Here, read this." You take the clipping about Mahoney from your desk drawer. "Mahoney is the man who sold your father the emerald."

Mark reads the clipping and turns pale. "Where did you get this?" he demands.

"Never mind that. The Indians who struck at Mahoney have come here. They attacked me in the woods this afternoon. Look!" You pull the dart from your pocket. Mark gives a violent start. "They're hiding in the woods behind the school, real Indians! We must go to the police in the village."

"No! No police, do you hear?" Mark insists. "This only makes the theft worse! If my father hears I have lost the jewel, I am done for! And stay out of my affairs!"

"Wouldn't your father understand, especially since you are now in danger?" you ask.

Mark smiles bitterly. "You don't know my father."

"Who's Becky?" you dare to ask.

"What did I tell you? I'm warning you to stay away!" Mark cries, flinging Becky's crumpled note toward the fireplace before leaving. ***Turn to 257.***

200

At the white house at 116 Elm Street, Bingley stops and gazes at the window. First, he studies the house and the surrounding neighborhood and then gives a low whistle. Suddenly he walks around the house, to a garden enclosed by a tall fence. You go behind the next house and creep up to the fence. Trees border the fence, and you move along, away from the house, and climb a tree, to get a good look. As you reach a sturdy branch, a very pretty girl of sixteen or seventeen comes into the garden from the house. Black hair and dark eyes heighten the pale cream of her skin. Behind the garden, the woods take over. The girl looks about nervously, then runs up to Bingley.

"My parents will be home at four," she says softly.

"Tomorrow at the clearing we'll have more time. Let's say three o'clock, lest we forget."

"Fine, Richard."

You recognize her as Becky Connoly, the daughter of a local mill-worker, a town beauty whom you once met with Mark at a restaurant in the village.

Bingley gathers her in his arms and they kiss. Their voices have a softness to them that startles you, something you haven't heard at the school. Bingley takes out the jewel box and gives it to her. Becky takes from the box a ring and exclaims in delight. They move to a stone bench further away. ***Pick a number and add your Observation bonus:***
- *If 2-5, turn to 347.*
- *If 6-12, turn to 158.*

201

You follow Mark to Becky Connoly's house in the village of Belton. He approaches the back of the house and calls up to Becky's window. Becky's face appears in the window for a moment, then moves away. You watch as she exits the house and leads Mark to the garden.

They pause in a corner of the garden.

"What are you doing here?" Becky asks, flushed.

"Do you so dislike seeing me, then?" says Mark, his face twisting with pain.

Becky sighs. "Mark, it's not that. You know how I feel about you. You shall always be very dear to me."

"But not like Richard."

"No, not like Richard," she admits. "I'm sorry. I love him very much. I wish you two could be friends — he cares about you. I care about you."

Mark winces, noticing the pendant around Becky's neck.

"Is that from him?"

"Yes, it's a gift from Richard."

"Very nice," says Mark. "Is he giving you many presents?"

"Too many!" Becky replies. "I don't really need them. The dear boy has been selling all of his valuables to buy me things."

Mark takes a breath, then asks: "Did he give you an emerald, too, by any chance?" *Check Clue NN.* **Pick a number and add your Observation bonus:**
- *If 2-7, turn to 327.*
- *If 8-12, turn to 123.*

202

After offering you a cup of tea, Holmes asks: "Who stole the Black River Emerald?"
- *If you accuse Mark Avery, turn to 212.*
- *If you accuse Oxy Oxfield, turn to 278.*
- *If you accuse Mr. Mueller, turn to 208.*
- *If you accuse Richard Bingley, turn to 203.*
- *If you accuse Muskrat Rafferty, turn to 205.*

203

Holmes nods sternly, disguising his attitude. "I see. Why do you accuse him?"

You breathlessly weave the tale of all you have learned about Richard Bingley and the Emerald.

"Illuminating, but cirumstantial," says Holmes, dismissing your deductions. *Turn to 348.*

204

The next day, after morning classes and lunch, Muskrat's father shows up at the school. Mr. Rafferty looks like his son, save that he is thirty years older and a bit meaner. Whiskers bristle from his chin; his furtive eyes seem to glance about for predators who might pounce on him from behind hedges and posts. He is well-dressed, but his brilliant necktie, shining pin, and glittering rings are flamboyant to the point of gaudiness. He is accompanied by a large, swarthy fellow with a formidable dark moustache, whom he introduces as "my associate, Mr. Lomax." Mr. Rafferty closets himself with his son in Muskrat's room. You amble past the door, hoping to eavesdrop, but the lumbering Lomax glares at you from beneath his black brows.

You go to your room, wondering how you could somehow overhear their conversation. From somewhere you hear laughter: it must be Langford and McSwain, the two students who live below you. You again hear their mocking laughter from the room below, as you do regularly every night before sleep, when they find a target for their jibes from among the other students. The laughter ascends and falls like an arpeggio. *Pick a number and add your Intuition bonus:*
- *If 2-6, turn to 216.*
- *If 7-12, turn to 344.*

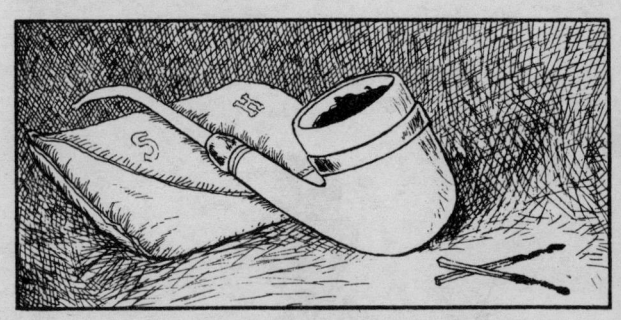

205

Holmes nods sternly, disguising his attitude. "I see. Why do you accuse him?"

You breathlessly weave the tale of all you have learned about Muskrat and the Emerald.

"Illuminating, but cirumstantial," says Holmes, dismissing your deductions.
- *If you have checked Clue L, turn to 209.*
- *Otherwise, turn to 348.*

206

In your room, your weary eyes begin to close. How much more of this can I take, you wonder.
- *If you have checked Clue N but not Clue NN, turn to 174.*
- *Otherwise, turn to 292.*

207

You light a lamp on low, and find the blotting paper on the desk. The blotting paper has these marks on it:

> Joe,
> I think you truly can no longer help me.
> You must leave this area. I will...
> ...submit to your blackmail. Do not cou...
> ...my promise to mother.
> Karl

Pick a number and add your Scholarship bonus:
- *If 2-7, turn 330.*
- *If 8-12, turn to 170.*

208

"I see," Holmes says, reaching for his pipe. "What physical evidence did you uncover, may I ask?"

You pause to review the clues you have gathered before replying.
- *If you have checked Clue R, turn to 222.*
- *If you have checked Clue EE, turn to 222.*
- *If you have checked Clues L and J, turn to 239.*
- *Otherwise, turn to 225.*

209

"You have done well to discover that old man Rafferty had possession of the Emerald," Holmes admits, lighting his pipe, "but that does not mean that he stole the gem, does it? Mightn't he have an accomplice?" *Turn to 348.*

210

Oxy loses you in the maze of dormitory hallways. Did he notice I was following him, you wonder. *Turn to 290.*

211

The branch breaks with a cracking sound. The points of the fence's slats reel up toward you as you fall. You manage to push off from the tree and land in the garden. You crumple to the ground, your ankle shooting pain. *Reduce your Athletics bonus by one for the remainder of this adventure.* Bingley walks toward you and stands towering above you. You slowly stand, your ankle throbbing. ***Turn to 262.***

212

Holmes nods sternly, disguising his attitude. "I see. Why do you accuse him?"

You breathlessly weave the tale of all you have learned about Mark and the Emerald.

"Illuminating, but cirumstantial," says Holmes, dismissing your deductions. ***Turn to 348.***

213

Downstairs you carefully count the rooms and come to the door of 215. You knock on the door and hear a high whine. Entering, you find a boy crying: Higby-Ross, from the fourth form. "What's the matter?" you ask, moving below the grate in the ceiling, over by the corner.

"Someone stole my music box," he whimpers. Tears stream down his cheeks. You succeed to some extent in deciphering the voices from beyond the grate as the boy hushes.

"Well, I'm afraid you can't come to Bighton," old man Rafferty says. He must mean "Brighton."

"Why not?" Muskrat whines.

Higby-Ross cries again, covering the old man's reply. You try to console him. "Well, maybe you'll find it tomorrow. Now hush."

The old man's voice comes down from the grate. "_____ is not safe. You can visit your mother in Shropshire."

"I hate Shropshire. I want to come with you."

"It's not safe, do you understand?" He says something you cannot make out and "...put you in danger! Now that's that!" *Check Clue I.*

Higby-Ross lets out a wail. "Without my box, I can't get to sleep! If I cannot sleep, I shall never study — and I shall never get out of here! Da' will never let me come home!" He drowns out the upstairs noises.

"Why can't you sleep?" you ask, perturbed.

"Oh, it sounds so stupid! You'll laugh," the boy whimpers.

"I promise I won't laugh."

"That's the only way I could get to sleep, by playing the box. We used to play the box at home. I hate it here! I shall never get home...!"

"We all hate it here," you say to console him, and return to your room. *Turn to 216.*

214

Later, as you're walking to Perkins Hall, you notice Richard Bingley heading into the woods.
- *If you follow him, turn to 138.*
- *Otherwise, turn to 223.*

215

The boulders lead you nowhere. As you disconsolately walk back toward the campus, you come upon a seldom-used path leading away from school. *Pick a number and add your Intuition bonus:*
- *If 2-9, turn to 273.*
- *If 10-12, turn to 281.*

216

Later, from your window you see Mr. Rafferty enter the administration building; shortly thereafter, the curtains to Mr. Mueller's office window close.
- *If you want to spy on them, pick a number and add your Athletics bonus:*
  - *If 2-6, turn to 160.*
  - *If 7-12, turn to 301.*
- *Otherwise, turn to 229.*

3

217

The shoeprints lead to the center of the clearing where they meet a different set of bootprints smaller and narrower, with the heel distinct from the sole, indicating a higher heel (and thus the footware of a girl). A rose, its deep crimson vibrating in the grey light, shines against the dark brown of the mud. The female bootprints and the shoe prints face each other in the center of the clearing.

The bootprints with the horizontal tread and a "W" on the heel take a more circuitous route to the clearing, first marking up an area behind a set of trees along the old cart-road, then an area behind a set of trees in the clearing. They emerge from behind the second set of trees and approach the other prints. The broad shoeprints turn and face them. Beside the facing set of prints, a muddy area shows the imprint of a fall. The shoe prints and the female bootprints go off together into the woods toward town, where the female bootprints came from. The bootprints with the tread return to the old cart-road. *Check Clue E.*

You try to figure out what it all means, imagining Holmes and his methods. *Pick a number and add your Intuition bonus:*
- *If 2-7, turn to 118.*
- *If 8-12, turn to 115.*

218

You walk to Belton School with some apprehension. As you approach the school grounds, a carriage hurriedly rattles past you. *Turn to 240.*

219

You walk to the address on Holmes' note, 18 Hagglethorp Road — but the address is that of a greengrocer's shop. As you're standing by the shop windows, peeking in, you are grabbed from behind and struck a fierce blow to the head. *Turn to 173.*

220

The branch cracks as you shimmy back toward the tree trunk. Prepared for the fall, you drop to the ground and land on your feet like a cat. You notice a figure — Bingley's — racing behind the fence and run toward the woods. As you reach the woods, Bingley opens the gate, and you hide behind a tree. *Pick a number and add your Artifice bonus:*
- *If 2-4, turn to 337.*
- *If 5-12, turn to 145.*

221

You examine the jewels and determine that they hold little value — zircon, onyx, amber, and the rest, glass. *Check Clue II. Turn to 236.*

222

"Excellent, dear boy!" Holmes cries, impressed. "You have evidence directly linking Headmaster Mueller to the Emerald. You have all the makings of a genuine detective!" *Turn to 237.*

223

When you get back to your room, you find it ransacked. Bedsheets lie heaped in the corner. Drawers are opened and sifted through. Mark's trunk is turned on its side, the contents spilling from its mouth like fruit from a horn of plenty. His expensive shirts lie strewn about the room. Suddenly Mark enters and looks wildly about.

"Mark, they want the jewel! You are in danger!" you cry. "Go to the constable in the village."

"Don't meddle in my affairs!" replies Mark, fuming. "If you haven't already."

"Mark, I am your friend! If I had the jewel, don't you think I'd give it to you? If I weren't your friend, would I have gone to Sherlock Holmes?"

"Sherlock Holmes? The detective?"

You show him the letter from Holmes. He reads it and crumples it in his hand.

"Even Holmes cannot help me now! I must find the emerald!" he cries wildly. "And if it wasn't you who took the emerald, how did — whoever it was — discover the false bottom to the trunk?"

"Anyone could have sneaked in here when we were gone," you deduce. "Look how many things have been stolen recently. Maybe they discovered the trunk's bottom while they were looking for something else to steal and sell. And when they found the strongbox, they only needed to get the key from you."

"I am lost!"

"Let me help you, Mark," you plead. "I am your best friend. Trust me."

"Until the emerald is found, I trust no one." Avery casts wildly about, his features haggard, and leaves.

You gloomily clean up the room and go to dinner. At the table behind you, you notice Oxy whispering to Muskrat. *Pick a number and add your Observation bonus:*
- *If 2-6, turn to 196.*
- *If 7-12, turn to 192.*

224

On your way to the station, you contemplate the loss of the key on the rugby field. What would Holmes have noticed that you have missed?

Holmes said to consider all those who have been told about the jewel, even Mr. Mueller, the headmaster. As the rugby coach, he too had gathered around Mark on the field. *Pick a number and add your Intuition Bonus:*
- *If 2-6, turn to 361.*
- *If 7-12, turn to 129.*

225

"Without physical evidence — clues, if you will — directly linking a person to the crime or to the Emerald, you have no case, dear boy," Holmes says, as if lecturing a class. "You have failed to uncover sufficient proof to successfully accuse anyone; no court in England would try a man for such a serious crime without evidence of motive, method and opportunity." *Turn to 237.*

226

On Friday, today, the students leave for the Christmas holidays. Walking to Perkins Hall, you notice Oxfield and Muskrat slip off together into the woods.
- *If you follow them, pick a number and add your Artifice bonus:*
  - *If 2-6, turn to 363.*
  - *If 7-12, turn to 289.*
- *If you do not follow them, turn to 193.*

227

"I didn't get that far in Latin class," you say. "Besides, I doubt that Joe Miller has a working familiarity with Latin, either, sir."

Mr. Mueller glares threateningly at you. "You'd be better off concentrating on your Latin than talking to the town drunkard." For the remainder of the tea, you catch him giving you sidelong glances. Perhaps Joe Miller was telling the truth. *Check Clue G. Turn to 135.*

228

You turn the knob, and the tumblers click. The metal door to the headmaster's safe opens. Inside, you find the Mark's opened strongbox and the key, but no emerald. *Check Clue R. Turn to 121.*

229

You decide to write a letter to Mr. Holmes telling him what you've discovered so far.
- *If you go to the telegraph office, turn to 103.*
- *Otherwise, turn to 214.*

230

You note that the bootprints with the W on the heel and horizontal ridges are on top of the other shoeprints. *Pick a number and add your Intuition bonus:*
- *If 2-5, turn to 144.*
- *If 6-12, turn to 306.*

231

You turn the corner and find that you've lost sight of him. For five minutes, you pace the street. Then Bingley emerges from a shop nearby.
- *If you follow him, turn to 200.*
- *Otherwise, turn to 223.*

232

After dinner, the school talent show is held. A blast of catcalls and sarcastic remarks greet students sufficiently vain or foolish to try their hands at performing. Muskrat comes on stage second and sings Irish ballads. Jeers and cheers from the crowd arise.

"A rat, do I smell a rat?"

Chants of "Musk! I smell musk!" come from the audience. In the middle of his ballad, "A Little Bit of Heaven Known as Mother," a sign drops from stage left. Muskrat stares at the sign, goes white, stops singing, and stumbles back, exiting stage right. You dash to the front of the auditorium and try to read the sign. *Pick a number and add your Observation bonus:*
- *If 2-8, turn to 364.*
- *If 9-12, turn to 166.*

233

You slip the note beneath a book on the desk as he throws himself on his bed. You remember how Mark took you home to his parent's estate for the Christmas holidays last year, how he introduced you to the most important boys at the school, and nominated you to join the Society of Five.

"Mark," you say, your voice quivering, "I'm your friend. You must believe me." He takes a stick from the firewood and cleans the mud off his boot, ignoring you. "Mark, I didn't take your emerald. I'm trying to help you. Listen to me — you're in great danger! The Indians who owned the jewel have come to reclaim it. That is why your father wants you to return it to him. Here." You take the clipping about Mahoney from your desk drawer and give it to him. "Mahoney is the man who sold your father the emerald."

Mark reads the clipping and turns pale. "Where did you get this?" he demands.

"Never mind that. The Indians who struck at Mahoney have come here to the school. They attacked me in the woods this afternoon. Look!" You pull the dart from your pocket. Mark gives a violent start. "They are hiding in the woods behind the school. We must go to the police in the village."

"No! No police, do you hear?" Mark insists. "This only makes the theft worse! If my father hears I have lost the jewel, I am done for."

"Wouldn't your father understand, especially since you're in danger?" you ask.

Mark smiles bitterly. "You don't know my father." He stands. "And stay well away from this business and out of my affairs!" He flings the stick toward the fireplace and leaves. *Turn to 257.*

234

You stumble against the pawnshop window. Bingley and the pawnshop clerk turn toward the window; you step back, hiding. Bingley and the clerk turn back to the items before them. A clarinet and snuff-boxes block the window where you stand, so you cannot discern what items the pawnbroker takes. *Turn to 317.*

235

You pay the man and are handed Holmes' letter. *Deduct 7 pence from your Money on your Character Record. Turn to 180.*

236

You search the box for the Black River Emerald but can't find it. The collection of childish items like marbles and a chunk of mica underlines Oxy's fascination with jewels. Beside the box, you find a book entitled "Famous Gems of the World." On page 54, you find a picture of the Black River Emerald. The picture is circled in red ink. *Check Clue LL.*

Suddenly, the door creaks open. Big as a bear, Oxy stands grinning malevolently at you. "Well, well. What have we here, a thief?" he says.

Muskrat, like a parasitic fish around a shark, comes up beside him.

"A boy going through my bureau," Oxy says, slowly approaching you, his hand curling into a fist. "A filthy foreigner and a thief, too. Too bad he hadn't heard they cut short Evening Study to save the lamp gas." As Muskrat squeals with delight, Oxy's fist flashes, and your chest goes cold with pain. "Rat, I think we shall have some fun."

Oxy lunges toward you. The shirts on the dresser fly as you are thrown backwards onto the bed.

"I'll wager he wishes he never left his own country. I'll wager he wants his old mum now!" Muskrat squeals.

At her mention you see your mother, waving and smiling at you as you left for school, and, despite the imminent blow from Oxy's fist, a sudden homesickness overwhelms you. Oxy brings you back to the present with a sharp rap to your shoulder. *Pick a number and add your Athletics bonus:*
- *If 2-8, turn to 179.*
- *If 9-12, turn to 372.*

237

"Think, dear boy," Holmes continues, blowing a cloud of blue smoke toward the ceiling. "How might Headmaster Mueller have obtained the Emerald? We know that he and all the other suspects had the opportunity to steal the key on the Rugby practice field that day that Mark Avery was knocked down. What method did Mueller employ to get the key?"
- *If you have checked Clues B and X, turn to 264.*
- *Otherwise, turn to 266.*

238

With a pounding heart, you notice the passenger staring out as the carriage thunders past: Mr. Rafferty!
- *If you approach Mr. Mueller's house, turn to 271.*
- *Otherwise, turn to 185.*

239

"What you have discovered provides a link between Headmaster Mueller and old man Rafferty, but it is not conclusive evidence that they stole or now have possession of the Emerald, don't you agree?" Holmes inquires.

You must agree. *Turn to 237.*

240

The carriage rattles up Mr. Mueller's drive. *Pick a number and add your Observation bonus:*
- *If 2-4, turn to 309.*
- *If 5-12, turn to 238.*

You approach the Headmaster, Mr. Mueller, the tea cup jittering in the saucer you're holding. His cruel, thin-lipped mouth, surmounted by a long, curved nose (like the beak of an eagle) flashes into a perfunctory smile. He seems preoccupied. You notice that his dark grey suit, though well-pressed, is worn and fraying, and the color faded at the elbows and knees.

"So how have you been, Master Rogers?" he inquires vacantly.

"Well, the afternoon has not been without interest."

"I am pleased we are keeping our students amused."

"I was accosted by the drunkard in town, a Mr. Miller."

He gives a violent start. "What did he want from you?"

"Oh, the usual," you reply anxiously. "Tuppence for beer."

"And what is of interest about that?"

"Not much. Except what he told me in exchange."

Mueller jumps again, as if slapped, but masters himself with a violent effort, his grim mouth loosening into a strange laugh which seems more menacing than his frown. "And what is that?"

"Oh, I promised to keep that a secret."

"You think your word to a drunkard is more important than that to me?"

"No, sir. But I gave my word."

Mr. Mueller smiles again broadly, as though to dismiss the affair. "Very good, lad. I am relieved to see that you are acquiring our sense of honor."

Rising, you walk away. Throughout the tea, you catch glimpses of the headmaster watching you askance. Perhaps Joe Miller was telling the truth. *Check Clue G. Turn to 135.*

242

You bring your heel down hard on Lomax's toe. He lets out a groan, and you struggle in his grasp. You kick him in the shins, and he hurls you roughly to the ground. Lomax hobbles toward you and you run, your arm aching, down the drive and to the main gate. The oaf limps after you a while, then gives up and turns back to Perkins Hall.
Turn to 229.

243

You hear the strange cries of birds off through the trees. As you make your way after Muskrat, the bird cries intensify and surround you. You look up in the trees and the sun's rays, piercing the forest gloom, blind you. Where are the birds? Muskrat moves away quickly and you follow.

Then you hear a whirr and feel a rush of air against your cheek. A sharp knock sounds against the tree beside you. A dart sticks into the trunk. What in the world!? You turn and see a small, painted figure running behind the trees to your left, as bird-cries echo through the forest. Indians in England!!?
- *If you chase the figure, turn to 272.*
- *If you examine the dart, turn to 294.*
- *If you follow Muskrat, turn to 313.*

244

When you reach the London station, you trail Mr. Rafferty and his associate in the crowd. Street vendors, costermongers, jugglers and beggars slow you with their pleas for a few bob. As you leave the station, you notice the flamboyant-dressed foreigner gesticulating angrily to a beleagered conductor, his flame-colored silk flashing brightly. "I, sir, left my baggage! I am Wilhelm Gottsriech Sigismond von Ormstein, Grand Duke.."

Beneath the great arch of the station entrance a quartet of Oxford students, perhaps under the influence of the brewmaster's art, stand singing boisterously in their straw boater hats.

Rafferty and Lomax take a hansom cab, and you hail the cab behind them. You follow them to Claridge's, one of the city's finest hotels. After Mr. Rafferty and his bodyguard have entered the hotel, you pay the driver two shillings and slip into the lobby. *Deduct two shillings from your Money on your Character Record.* Mr. Rafferty registers at the desk; later, he and Lomax stroll into the dining room. They sit eating at a well laid table of roast beef, Yorkshire pudding, stewed tomatoes and fresh rolls, washed down with ale. Your stomach pulls — you haven't eaten for hours, but the menu is far too expensive. On the street, you find a cheap restaurant opposite, and eat a greasy mutton pie for one shilling, sixpence at a window facing the hotel. *Deduct the cost of the meal from your Money on your Character Record.* You watch the hotel as evening descends and the streetlamps are lit.

Mr. Rafferty exits the hotel alone and gets into a hackney coach. You can't find another cab, and run after Rafferty's. At a fruit stand, a horse stands tied up to a fruit cart near the market down the street. *Pick a number and add your Athletics bonus:*
- *If 2-8, turn to 252.*
- *If 9-12, turn to 268.*

245

You don't notice anything in particular about the prints.
If you follow the prints, turn to 217.
Otherwise, turn to 311.

246

You hit the wall heavily and pass out. *Pick a number and add your Athletics bonus:*
- *If 2-5, turn to 367.*
- *If 6-12, turn to 188.*

247

After considerable effort and ingenuity, you reconstruct most of the letter, and read:

Dear Mark:

The matter at hand has assumed an importance far beyond what I have told you. Certain events have made your possession of the stone an extreme hazard to you, and to myself as well. It is of utmost importance that you bring the emerald home with you when you come on Friday, and that you do this with utmost secrecy. If I could come to you, I would, but that would only cast both of us in greater danger. I will explain when I see you. I do not mean to alarm you, but while you have the stone with you, you are in considerable danger. Be circumspect. Guard the jewel closely, and keep all in secret. I have placed my trust in you with this, and I am confident that as an Avery you shall merit that trust. I look forward to seeing you for this and...

You recognize Mark's father's seal on the envelope. *Check Clue C. Turn to 284.*

248

You study the cigar butt for a moment longer. From the aroma and the distinctive counterclockwise roll of the tobacco leaf, you note that the cigar is a Galliardi brand, a particularly expensive cigar from Italy. *Pick a number and add your Observation bonus:*
- *If 2-8, turn to 217.*
- *If 9-12, turn to 249.*

249

Galliardi cigars are the brand smoked by Richard Bingley, a fact you noticed when you met him at the train station. *Check Clue KK. Turn to 217.*

250

Walking down the Main Street, you meet Richard Bingley on the street.

"Are you going back up to school? I'll walk with you," you suggest.

"I have a few errands to do," he says, trying to rush ahead of you.

You think of the dart in the forest, and the vines that bound you. "But it's dangerous in the woods, even on the road."

"Dangerous?" he scoffs. "What do you mean?"

"There are Indians in the forest," you blurt out. "They've come for the emerald."

"Don't be silly! You don't believe in that nonsense, do you? Really, Rogers, I thought you were one of the bright ones here."

"They shot at me with darts!"

"Have you gone off your bean? Oh, I see — you're having a laugh," Bingley concludes, smiling. "Well, I must be off. These errands will take time. I have some shopping to do, and other odd bits as well."

"I don't mind. I'd like to come with you."

"I'd rather walk alone!" Bingley's face bursts into a fury suddenly. Then he smiles. "Sorry. I just have this aching need, old boy, to be by myself. You understand. I shall see you at dinner, eh?" And he hurries off down the street.

Something about his manner bothers you, and you follow Bingley at a distance. He turns the corner into another street. *Pick a number and add your Artifice bonus:*
- *If 2-4, turn to 231.*
- *If 5-12, turn to 198.*

251

You reach the clearing and hide behind a great oak. *Pick a number and add your Observation bonus:*
- *If 2-5, turn to 100.*
- *If 6-12, turn to 258.*

2

252

You untie the horse's reins, leap onto the cart and wheel off after Rafferty's coach, apples and melons tumbling from behind you; the horse rears and shies. Suddenly the cart's wheel hits the curb, and the cart veers across the road and crashes into a steetlamp. Melons, apples, pears, and lemons litter the street, their reds and greens and yellows shining in a tropical display beneath the flickering lamp. An apple rolls slowly down the sidewalk, bouncing against the flagstones. Disconsolate, you hurry from the scene of the accident, eager to escape before a constable nabs you, and rush to Baker Street to report to Holmes. *Turn to 297.*

253

"It was Oxy who stole the Emerald!" you cry. *Turn to 365.*

254

From out of nowhere and moving like panthers, Indians surround you. A dart hits your shoulder. As you spin to grab it, another dart pierces your leg. A sudden faintness overcomes you. Then a dart hits you in the back. The ground reels up toward you as you pass out. *Turn to 368.*

255

You put down the letter and find Mark's father's seal on the envelope. Though you can only make out some of it, from what you can decipher and from Mark's desperation and his cry of "Give me the emerald!" you realize that his father must want the jewel from Mark, and that Mark would suffer greatly in his father's affection if he cannot return the emerald to him. *Check Clue C. Turn to 284.*

256

Lomax stands and points a finger at you. Jumping from your seat, you brush past the old lady in the seat beside yours and race down to the next car. Lomax runs after you, calling out: "Thief!" You race into the next carriage and run into a brown uniform. The train attendant, a tall, ruddy gentleman with blue eyes and florid cheeks, grabs you and holds you by your coat. "Going somewhere, lad?"

Pick a number and add your Communication bonus:
- *If 2-6, turn to 134.*
- *If 7-12, turn to 323.*

257

Catching your breath, you pause to consider what course of action to take.

- *If you have checked Clue D, turn to 328.*
- *Otherwise, turn to 135.*

258

Hand in hand, Becky Conolly and Richard Bingley enter the clearing. He takes from his pocket a billfold, and from the billfold, two ten-pound notes. He hands them to Becky along with a map.

"They will be looking for us together, so we'd better travel alone," Richard counsels his sweetheart. "I shall meet you in Paris, at this hotel, on Tuesday evening. Here are your train tickets, and this is the ticket for the channel crossing. Here is the address of a friend of mine in Paris, whom you must contact, oui?"

"Richard, your family — " says Becky, trembling.

The boy's expression hardens. "If they don't approve of you, then they're not worth regretting."

"But your father, your mother — your home!"

"We will make a new home," Richard says softly.

"But the money — your inheritance..."

"Fortunes have been made before. I just hope that you don't care — "

"Oh, Richard, how could you even think..." She kisses him. "I am certain that one day your father will welcome us into his home."

"You mustn't count on that."

"You are going to be Sir Richard Bingley the Fourth!" She kisses him again, tossling his hair. "Sir Richard Bingley."

"Are the arrangements clear?"

"They are."

"Oh, this." Richard hands her a gold ring. "We'll hold the ceremony in Paris, agreed?"

As they kiss, you decide you have seen enough and head back to school. *Check Clue V. Turn to 232.*

259

You bring the shelf of canned goods down on Lomax with a crash. He stumbles back against the counter as you rush to the street. You race to the fruit wagon, untie the horse, and leap up onto the cart. Flicking the reins, you take off down the street. Behind you, Lomax points you out to the man in the bowler hat, who leaps into a carriage and takes off after you. As you turn the corner, the cart veers sideways, leaning uneasily toward the right wheel.

The carriage slowly catches up to you. Houses spin by. You careen through a puddle, and the dark water sprays yellow in the streetlamp. ***Pick a number and add your Artifice bonus:***
- *If 2-8, turn to 162.*
- *If 9-12, turn to 269.*

260

The man lunges toward you. You duck, and he tumbles with a cry onto the street. Seizing the reins, you turn a corner and take a circuitous route back to the shop.

Just as you arrive, Rafferty emerges from the shop and takes a cab across town, losing you in heavy carriage traffic. Discouraged, you leave the wagon and walk back to 221B Baker Street. ***Turn to 197.***

261

You pass an hour watching Rafferty wolf down kidney pies and cider. He comes out of the restaurant and strolls contentedly to the platform to catch the train that stops at Belton, among other places. What a waste of time! *Turn to 338.*

262

"What are you doing here?" Bingley demands. He turns to Becky. "Spying, he's been spying on us."

His hand grips your shirt, strangling you. His fist flashes, and a dark cold grips your chest. Your cheeks sting as his hand, open, moves back and forth, slapping you.

"Spying on us. So you're on Mark's team after all!" Bingley sneers.

"No, I'm just trying to find the jewel," you cry. "I thought you'd taken it. Mark's in danger."

"What do you mean?" Becky's asks, approaching you.

"Mark's in danger from the tribe of Indians who orignally owned the emerald. He must find the jewel, and fast!"

Bingley sneers and laughs. "And you think I took his precious jewel?" he snorts.

"I have no idea. But you're his enemy."

Bingley smiles bitterly. "If that's his version."

"Richard, we must help him," Becky pleads.

"It was he who declared war." The fist moves back and comes toward you. Pain shoots across your face. "Sending his filthy spies."

"Where did you get the money for those gifts?" you manage to ask.

Becky turns to him. "Yes, Richard, where?"

"I don't explain myself to spies," Bingley snaps. "Now get going or I shall thrash you senseless!" The fist flashes again, and your shoulder throbs with pain. You limp towards the woods, your ankle almost buckling beneath you, and hobble back to school. *Turn to 223.*

263

You set out at a brisk pace to find the caves Muskrat was heading towards through the woods, scanning the trees for the Indians. Frightened, you race through the woods toward the cliffs. As you reach the rugged area, you search for the landmark you had noted.
- *If the landmark was five large boulders in a pile, turn to 215.*
- *If the landmark was a waterfall, turn to 150.*
- *If the landmark was a red rock face, turn to 331.*

264

"Mr. Mueller was an amateur magician," you remind Holmes. "He relished picking pockets, and I recall the curious circular motions he made over Mark on the Rugby field that day."

"Excellent!" Holmes cries. *Turn to 274.*

265

After a long jaunt, you reach the edge of Belton Village. You wonder if you should go to the village constable with the dart, but remember Mark's opposition to such an action.

On Main Street, Joe Miller, the local drunkard, always begging a few bob for a mug, approaches. He has a vile appearance and is coarsely clad, with a colored shirt protruding through the rent in his coat.

"A few bob for a man in need, eh?" His grizzled stubble seem to scratch your face as he lunges unstably toward you. His breath burns against your skin, and you blush. You mutter that you can't help him, and he grabs your coat sleeve. "You think you're so high and mighty, you fine young men in your fancy garb. So high and mighty. Don't get me to laughing. You fancy young men think you're so dandy. Ha! My brother will teach you! Beat you senseless. Don't put on airs with me! If you knew who my brother was, you wouldn't slip by so quick!"
• *If you talk to Miller, turn to 339.*
• *Otherwise, turn to 283.*

266

After you falter, Holmes sighs and says: "As far as you have ascertained, all the suspects had ample opportunity and employed no special method to steal the Emerald." *Turn to 274.*

267

You grab the rail running around the top of the carriage (where the luggage rests) and settle onto the axle below just as the carriage takes off.

The carriage speeds and rattles to the station. You jump off as the carriage slows down. Losing yourself among the crowd at the station, you stand by the ticket office and watch Rafferty buying tickets for London.
• *If you take the train to London, turn to 190.*
• *Otherwise, turn to 104.*

268

You untie the horse, leaping onto the cart and wheeling after Rafferty's cab, apples and melons tumbling from behind you. The horse reponds to your grasp on the reins. A bobby's shrill whistle sounds behind you — he loses ground as he gives chase. Rafferty's coach stops at an intersection, and you pull up well behind him.

You continue following him to one of the filthiest streets of a dark London slum. Suddenly Rafferty pays the driver of the coach and exits into a greengrocer's shop. *Pick a number and add your Observation bonus:*
* *If 2-6, turn to 329.*
* *If 7-12, turn to 128.*

269

An idea strikes you: mount the horse ahead of you and disconnect the cart! Holding the reins, you crawl across the cart's shafts running alongside the horse. *Pick a number and add your Athletics bonus:*
* *If 2-6, turn to 334.*
* *If 7-12, turn to 291.*

270

You notice a closet door in the corner and creep toward it. The handle of the office door turns, and the door creaks open. You enter the closet and pull the door shut behind you.

Another light goes on in the office. You hear Mueller moving about, muttering to himself. He sits down at his desk. The pounding of the typewriter comes from the desk. He pulls the sheet from the machine and takes out another. You hear the scratching of his quill pen on the paper, and the blotting paper being used. The chair squeaks, then footsteps move to the door. The office door opens, creaks and closes, and the footsteps recede down the hall. You open the closet door.
* *If you leave Mueller's office, turn to 121.*
* *Otherwise, pick a number and add your Intuition bonus:*
  * *If 2-5, turn to 330.*
  * *If 6-12, turn to 207.*

271

You creep up to Mueller's house and peek in the window. *Pick a number and add your Observation bonus:*
* *If 2-5, turn to 308.*
* *If 6-12, turn to 315.*

272

The figure runs deeper into the woods, hopping vines and roots like a rabbit. Amid the cry of birds, you dash after him. Periodically you lose sight of him, only to see a streak of color beyond the trunks in the distance. *Pick a number and add your Athletics bonus:*
- *If 2-7, turn to 157.*
- *If 8-12, turn to 349.*

273

You walk up the overgrown, winding path but cannot locate a cave. Disconsolate, you head back toward the school and your room. *Turn to 353.*

274

"Now, did Mr. Mueller have a motive?" Holmes inquires.
- *If you have checked Clue P, turn to 286.*
- *If you have checked Clue Z, turn to 286.*
- *If you have checked Clue Y, turn to 312.*
- *If you have checked Clue Q, turn to 312.*
- *Otherwise, turn to 299.*

275

You follow Oxy to the Pillars, a set of columns behind the administration building, and hide behind a pillar. *Turn to 116.*

276

Unable to locate the Emerald, you decide to give up and return to school. *Turn to 353.*

277

Muskrat rushes from the cave, and races past you into the woods. Oxy runs after him, cursing, as you hide along the rock wall. Oxy's oaths ring though the woods as they run off. Taking advantage of their absence, you search the cave again for the Emerald, and not finding it, set out toward school. *Turn to 159.*

278

Holmes nods sternly, disguising his attitude. "I see. Why do you accuse him?"

You breathlessly weave the tale of all you have learned about Oxy and the Emerald.

"Illuminating, but cirumstantial," says Holmes, dismissing your deductions. ***Turn to 348.***

279

You struggle through the crowd after Muskrat. You slowly catch up to him, staying far enough behind that he won't notice you. He walks into the train station and sits at one of the station's restaurants. You notice a group of shabbily dressed men smoking and laughing in a corner of the station, a tinker with his wheel, and two policemen flirting with a nanny. Watching the restaurant, you approach the tinker and idly watch the wheel spin against a knife blade.
- *If you return to Holmes' flat, turn to 338.*
- *If you wait for Muskrat, turn to 261.*

280

You duck and the shovel hits Oxy on the arm. He buckles with pain. You push past him and rush out the door.

In the safety of your locked room, you contemplate Oxy's actions. If he is guilty, where is the Black River Emerald? You fall asleep reading Shakespeare's "Hamlet." ***Turn to 204.***

Climbing the path, you discover and enter the cave. The darkness blinds you. Slowly you can make out a gleam at your feet: silverware. You pick up a fork. The silverware belongs to Belton School and is a fine old set: knives, forks, spoons, a serving platter, a tea pot and more. Beyond them lie watches, including Maloney's silver watch, reported stolen earlier in the year, and the Walrus's grandfather's watch and chain, stolen the Spring before.

Beyond them, deeper inside the shallow cave lie other objects reported stolen over the last three years: tie clips, cufflinks, a pile of silk shirts, five overcoats, and three sets of luggage. So it was Muskrat who stole the boys' property over the last three years, you conclude. *Check Clue T.* You wonder why Muskrat hasn't sold the goods after stealing them. Perhaps he was going to save them and sell them when he left school, using the funds as his entry to a professional career. Or perhaps he is a different kind of rat, a pack rat — a lesser dragon hoarding his lair.

You wonder how many students sacrificed their weekends, sat through the hours of lectures in the chapel, and then had to suffer again at the hands of their parents for having lost the items, because of Muskrat's curious habit. And how does he plan to get the treasure away from school, you wonder — especially with Headmaster Mueller's order that all luggage of leaving students must be searched (because of the theft of the Emerald). You search the area for the jewel. *Pick a number and add your Observation bonus:*
- *If 2-8, turn to 276.*
- *If 9-12, turn to 369.*

282

You approach Headmaster Mueller, the tea cup jittering in the saucer you're holding.

"Joe says hello," you tell him.

"Joe? Joe who?"

"Joe Miller."

Mueller gives a violent start and glares at you. "Who is this Joe Miller?"

"Joe Miller, the drunkard in town. He said he needs money."

Mueller jumps again, as if struck, but masters himself with an extreme effort, his grim mouth loosening into a smile, which seems more menacing than his frown. "What can you be talking about?"

"I only relate what he said."

"Do not pay attention to riffraff, lad! From a fellow like that, what you buy is not worth a farthing. *Caveat emptor*, Master Rogers."

Pick a number *and add your Scholarship bonus:*
- *If 2-5, turn to 227.*
- *If 6-12, turn to 163.*

283

You reach the post office and climb the steps with relief.

As you send a telegram and a letter to Holmes mentioning the Indians, the man behind the counter stares at the address.

"That's odd. We have just received a letter from that address... Are you David Rogers?"

"Right."

"Here's a letter for you. Just come with the latest post. That will be six pence for the telegram and a penny for the letter."

- *If you do not have any money, turn to 316.*
- *Otherwise, turn to 235.*

284

The fear and anger you feel toward Mark dissolve with the knowledge of his plight, turning into compassion and anxiety. The jewel must be found. You try to think how Mr. Holmes would reason. If you have eliminated all the impossibilities, that which remains, however improbable, must be the case. All seem possible suspects: Muskrat, Oxfield, Richard, even Mr. Mueller.

You compose a telegram to Holmes, along with a letter describing what you've discovered so far. Perhaps he has completed his other case and can come to your aid. *Turn to 130.*

285

After lunch, you have an hour until Geometry class.
- *If you have checked Clue AAA, turn to 177.*
- *Otherwise, turn to 142.*

286

"I learned that the School is deeply in debt," you reply, "and simple observation reveals the physical decline of the buildings." *Turn to 305.*

287

You try to catch the numbers as Mueller turns the knob of the safe, but cannot quite make them out. *Turn to 296.*

288

Oxy lunges at you, swinging wildly. You duck and shove him, and he falls heavily against the clothes trunk. Then the oaf stands, dizzy and bewildered, and like a bull who's been stung, snorts with rage. Angry, he reaches down among the silverware, picks up a fork, and rushes you, jabbing the air with the fork.

You grab a silver tea-service tray and a ladle. The fork clangs against the tray and bounces off. You parry Oxy's thrusts with your ladle; Muskrat picks up a silver teapot and sends the silver cylinder flying at you. The teapot ricochets off the cave wall with a clang. Frustrated, Oxy throws the fork away, and he and Muskrat rush you. You dodge them, and Oxy crashes into Muskrat, knocking them both down.

"You bleeding idiot!" Muskrat whines.

"Shut your mouth, or I'll — " Oxy roars.

"Clumsy hulk!"

As they argue, you sneak away.

"Fool!" Muskrat cries, standing.

"Where did he go?"

"He got away..."

You run into the woods and hide until they have given up finding you. *Turn to 159.*

289

You discreetly follow Muskrat Rafferty and Oxy to a cave they call "Muskrat's." Rafferty lights a gas lantern. An eerie glow chills you as you crouch behind a rock.

"Where's the money?" Oxy growls. ***Pick a number and add your Observation bonus:***
- *If 2-5, turn to 151.*
- *If 6-12, turn to 351.*

290

You pause to consider your options, limited as they are.
- *If you steal into Headmaster Mueller's office after lights out, turn to 161.*
- *Otherwise, turn to 174.*

291

You mount the horse, and, leaning over, pull the straps. The cart zigzags crazily behind you as the horse pulls away. The carriage swerves, crashes into the cart, and topples over. Unhurt, you turn the corner and head by a circuitous route back to the shop.

Just as you arrive, Rafferty emerges from the shop and takes a cab across town, losing you in the heavy carriage traffic. Disappointed, you ride to 221B Baker Street. *Turn to 197.*

After a tedious morning of Mathematics, Latin and the Classics (and no word from Holmes), you go to lunch. As you sit to eat, there is a sudden scream from the kitchen. Mrs. MacClaran, the cook, runs from the kitchen, shaking.

"A devil, a painted devil!" she screams.

"Whatever can you mean, Mrs. MacClaran?" Mr. Quigley, the Latin teacher, asks.

"Why sirr," she says, her Scottish brogue thickening, " 'tis a devil, as naked as the day! Or a MacDonough gone mad, come to revenge his clan. He had the strangest feathered tartan painted something fierce-like!" The poor woman faints.

When you and Mr. Quigley run into the kitchen, you find only an open window and a jar of meal missing from the pantry shelf.

The overbearing Muskrat then regales you with his selection for the up-coming talent show: "A Little Bit of Heaven Known as Mother." He is greeted with a round of sarcastic applause, which fades as Sir Richard Bingley enters and walks through the dining room. From his spats to his gold-rimmed spectacles, his dress is orthodox and

[7]

elegant to the last degree. Yet his face is drawn and haggard, his cheeks lined and pinched toward his aristocratic Roman nose. Sir Richard approaches your table, summons his son, and they leave the room together.
• *If you follow them, turn to 152.*
• *Otherwise, turn to 285.*

293

After an uneventful train ride to Belton Village, you take a coach back to school. Other students returning from the weekend gather at the gates. Melancholy and a sense of something almost approaching doom steal over you as you pass through the gates to Belton School. Beyond the gateway the old trees shoot their brances in a somber tunnel over your head as the carriage wheels are hushed by leaves on the drive.

You ride up to the main building, Perkins Hall, a large stone edifice, very old at the center, newer at the wings, with towering Tudor chimneys, and a lichen-spotted, high-pitched roof of Horsham slabs. The building is sinking into a dilapidated condition, the neglect even more obvious in the more recent wings than the original stone hall. The front steps are worn into curves by the feet of generations of schoolboys, and the ancient tiles on the portico floor, marked with the Belton coat of arms —a dormant owl clutching a quill pen above a field of swords, argent — are dulled from the ceaseless beatings of winter rain. Within, the ceilings are laid with heavy oaken beams, and the uneven floors sag and moan. An odor of age and decay pervade the whole school.

MAP of BELTON SCHOOL

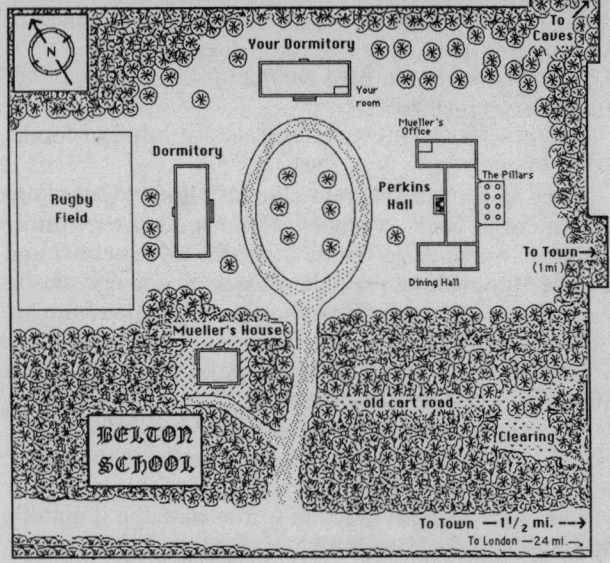

You shuffle with the others to the dining room, a dark wood-panelled hall of shadow and gloom. The room is a long chamber with a step separating the dais (where the masters sit) from the lower area reserved for the students. At one end a minstrels' gallery overlooks the room. Black beams cross above your head, with a smoke-darkened ceiling beyond them. With rows of flaring lamps to light it and the students' boisterous hubbub, the hall can sometimes assume the color and rude hilarity of an old-time banquet. But tonight with the lamps dim, and the prospect of another week of discipline ahead, the hall seems somber. A line of headmasters' portraits along the walls seems to keep watch over the diners as the food is served.

"So have we polished our performances for Thursday's Talent Night?" Muskrat shouts to the table.

"I would not even go near it," Richard Bingley sneers with his aristocratic lilt. "And please spare us your rendition of 'A Little Bit of Heaven Known as Mother,' as a favor, old sport."

"That, your majesty, is the best performance of the lot," Muskrat sneers.

"That does not qualify as a compliment, I should like to note," Bingley adds.

"What is this rot?" Oxy cries, his mouth full of food, letting his fork fall.

"Good God!" Bingley edges the food around his plate with his fork. "Liver and cauliflower — and now this."

A curious grey mess resembling mortar — oatmeal is perhaps the best guess — lies on your plate. The meals have been getting worse for a month, the lamps dimmer, the mood gloomier.

"Perhaps this is a Literature assignment, researching 'Robinson Crusoe,'" you suggest, nodding toward the oatmeal. "They're giving us the real flavor of the book."

"Even dear old Robbie ate better than this," Oxy mutters.

"I wonder what our dear masters are having tonight," Bingley says, and cranes toward the dais, where different food is served to the teachers. "Only mutton stew. They're slipping as well."

Muskrat scoops up a spoonful of the oatmeal. "I read in my 'Greek Glories' today that this bloke Archimedes invented the catapult, which helped win a war. Now that

I could enjoy researching." Muskrat pounds the handle of the spoon and launches a large dab of the grey mess, hitting Oxy in the face. "Research!" Muskrat cries, and launches a dab at Bingley as the table bursts into laughter and applause. "Research!" Spoons are lifted at the cue, and the grey mess flies.

The riot spreads down the long table. Even one of the tutors is seen launching great dollops of the mess with his serving spoon. Fists pound the table tops and a chant of "Roast beef, roast beef" fills the hall, as the masters come down from the dais. "My father is paying money for this." Bingley says. "What became of 'Rich, wholesome, meals, elegantly served...'"

Eventually Headmaster Mueller enters the dining hall amid the riot. The hall quiets. You notice Muskrat slip to the kitchen.

"What seems to be the cause of this disturbance?" Mr. Mueller demands of the senior master.

Muskrat enters from the kitchen with a fresh plate of

the grey food, and brings it up to Mr. Mueller. Smiles pass from student to student. In his most insolent tone, Muskrat whines: "Sir, we've been keeping your dinner warm. So delicious we thought you'd like a plate." Smiles and titters flit around the hall.

Mueller looks down at the food, and frowns. "I am not hungry at the moment, Master Rafferty. Take your seat." He turns to the diners. "You will have no dessert. Otherwise, we will overlook this incident." Then he exits the hall.

Later, back at your dormitory, your room is a freezing cave of gloom. You light a fire with the last of the firewood, and sit wondering if Mark will ever speak to you again. His new boots, with a W tread mark and parallel horizontal ridges across the bottom, lie opposite you beneath the bed. They seem to mock you, for he had taken you shopping in London, purchasing the boots at Harris' Bootery in the Strand and buying you a jacket at a nearby clothier. You'd shared sweet hot cross buns at the Bun Shop beside Harris's, and taken the underground to the show at the Paladium. When you tried to pay for the tickets, he waved you off with: "I'm dripping with funds, the family is simply dripping." You sit wondering if you will ever find the jewel and recover his friendship.

As you sit quietly, Mark enters with a letter and goes to his desk. He has a broad handsome face, his freckles reflecting his mother's Irish lineage. His friendly features now have only hostility and disdain written on them. He throws himself into a chair, rips open the envelope, and reads the letter. You recognize the return address as his father's. Mark's lips purse, his face turns white. He flings the letter toward the fireplace and springs at you, knocking you against the wall. His hands grip your throat; you choke, gasping for breath. Mark's eyes seem to scald you with hatred. "Give me the emerald, you filthy thief!" he cries, his face wild with anxiety. You feel yourself blacking out. ***Pick a number and add your Athletics bonus:***
- *If 2-6, turn to 246.*
- *If 7-12, turn to 362.*

294

You pull the feathered dart from the tree. *Pick a number and add your Observation bonus:*
- *If 2-5, turn to 132.*
- *If 6-12, turn to 318.*

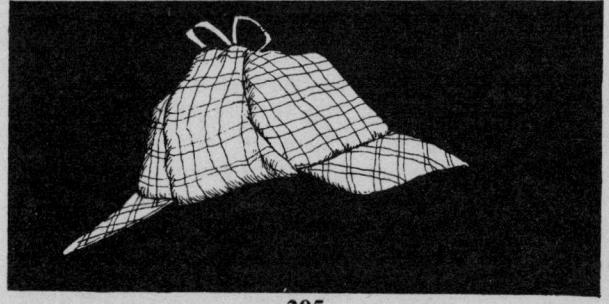

295

You limp slowly to the train station as the train pulls away. Having lost Mr. Rafferty's trail, you glumly buy a ticket back to Belton Village, feeling that you have bitten off more than you could chew. *Turn to 250.*

296

The headmaster takes a bottle of cognac from the safe, locks the safe, and pours two glasses. Mueller and Mr. Rafferty raise their glasses and drink a solemn toast. *Check Clue J.*

Suddenly, out of nowhere, a hand grabs you by the scruff of the neck, and pulls you from the window ledge. You kick and struggle! The bullish Mr. Lomax glares at you glares at you beneath his black brows. "Caught a fish, 'ave we? And I'll be wagerin' Mr. Rafferty will take an interest in you. You're fooling with the wrong type, boy."

"So you'd best not tell him when I get away," you taunt him. "Rafferty wouldn't take kindly to your incompetence."

The bludger laughs, his black brows shining. "Thanks for the suggestion, mate, but you ain't going to get away."

Pick a number and add your Artifice bonus:
- *If 2-7, turn to 242.*
- *If 8-12, turn to 172.*

297

"M'boy!" Watson greets you at the door. "My heavens, but you're a bit worse for wear. Come in, come in, and rest yourself! I'm afraid I must be off, though. Message from Holmes — he's on the scent again. How's the emerald affair? No, please, don't move. You look positively haggard. You must stay here tonight and rest. Holmes has gone and won't be home at least till tomorrow night, if I read this right. You may retire upon the couch. Slept there a number of times myself — much better than an Afghan mountainside, eh? Ring for Mrs. Hudson and order some broth or whatever you like. Oh, by the way, Holmes has a street number for you on that Rafferty scoundrel — it's on the desk. Must run." And he dashes off.

Mrs. Hudson cooks you a fine meal of steak and potatoes, then gives you fresh sheets and towels. You scribble a note to Holmes, explaining what you've discovered so far.

The next day, you arise early.

- *If you go to the address on Holmes' note, turn to 219.*
- *If you take the train to Belton, turn to 218.*

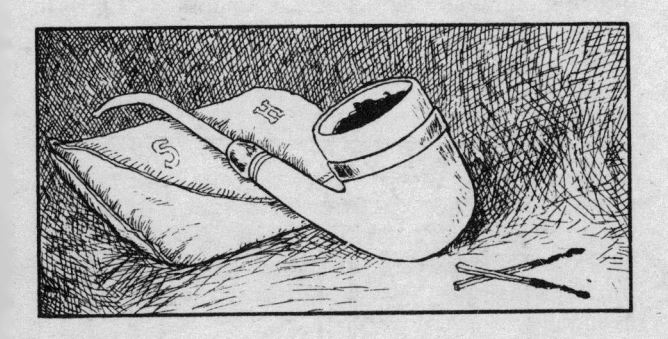

298

You notice a closet door in the corner and creep toward it. The handle of the office door turns, and the door creaks open. Realizing that you cannot reach the safety of the closet in time, you throw yourself beneath the huge desk. Another light goes on in the office. You hear Mueller moving about, muttering to himself. He sits at his desk, his feet beside you, his left shoe near your right hand. The pounding of the typewriter above you sounds like horsehooves on a bridge. You try to stifle your fear. Mueller mutters to himself, then pulls the sheet from the typewriter and takes another. You hear the scratching of his quill pen on the paper and the blotting paper being used. His shoes move away as Mueller stands. Footsteps make their way through the office door and recede down the hall.
- *If you leave Mueller's office, turn to 121.*
- *Otherwise, pick a number and add your Intuition bonus:*
  - *If 2-8, turn to 330.*
  - *If 9-12, turn to 207.*

299

"Without evidence as to motive," Holmes reminds you, "proving criminal intent is next to impossible." **Turn to 305.**

300

As you catch your breath, Holmes sighs, laying down his pipe. "I'm afraid we cannot assist you at present. I have a most important matter to attend to. I would suggest the local constabulary."

"That would be the surest way to lose Mark's friendship!" you reply, aghast at Holmes' counsel. "They would alert his father. When Mark discovered that the jewel was stolen, he insisted that Mueller not call in the police, and Mueller — I suppose to keep the school free of scandal — obliged him."

"Hum. If we can, we shall try to visit you there, but I'm afraid that for now, you are on your own," Holmes concludes. "But you must write me daily and describe whatever you find. I will put my head to the matter and make a few discreet inquiries. Perhaps you shall hear from me by post. And now we must be off, Watson." *Pick a number and add your Observation Bonus:*
- *If 2-6, turn to 361.*
- *If 7-12, turn to 340.*

301

You run to the administration building. Lifting yourself on to the window ledge, you peer through a crack in the curtains. Mr. Rafferty hands Mueller an envelope. Mueller takes the envelope and turns to open the safe behind his desk. *Pick a number and add your Observation bonus:*
- *If 2-8, turn to 287.*
- *If 9-12, turn to 310.*

302

Near the bootprints, the butt of a thin cigar lies beside a tree. *Check Clue UU. Pick a number and add your Observation bonus:*
- *If 2-7, turn to 127.*
- *If 8-12, turn to 139.*

303

After considerable effort you reconstruct some of the letter and read:

...matter at hand has assumed an... Certain events... made your possession of the stone..extreme hazard to you, and to myself... It is of utmost importance that you bring the emerald home... you do this ...could come to you... will explain ....secret...confident that as an Avery... merit that trust...

You recognize Mark's father's seal on the envelope. *Check Clue C. Turn to 284.*

304

You recall that Richard Bingley and Becky had set their appointment for three o'clock at the clearing. Your watch reads 2:15.
- *If you go to the clearing, turn to 251.*
- *Otherwise, turn to 232.*

305

Holmes sighs, and as you stir uncomfortably, says: "All in all, this theft provides an interesting if simple puzzle. Putting the pieces together is a pleasurable, if elemental, exercise."

"I still don't understand," you say.

- *If you want to play this adventure again without hearing Holmes' explanation of the crime, turn to the Prologue and begin again.*
- *If you want to hear Holmes' explanation of the crime, turn to 332.*

306

You deduce that the maker of the ridged bootprints must have followed the maker of the shoeprints. *Turn to 144.*

307

You purchase a ticket for two shillings, get on the train with Becky and find a seat behind her. *Deduct the fare from your Money on your Character Record.*

She takes the train to London, an enjoyable trip. She seems very fidgety and almost flies out of the train at Victoria Station. A flower vender approaches you with her wares and will not be put off; by the time you escape her, Becky has disappeared into the crowds. You kick a lamppost in annoyance, and the vender casts you a startled glance and moves off.

The school will be closed by the time you get back, so you decide to leave the station and walk to 221B Baker Street, where you must be prepared to present your solution of the theft to Mr. Holmes. *Turn to 202.*

308
Just my luck, you think — the curtains are closed! *Turn to 185.*

309
You notice the passenger staring out as the carriage thunders past, but you cannot quite tell who he is.
- *If you approach Mr. Mueller's house, turn to 271.*
- *Otherwise, turn to 185.*

310
You note the numbers as Mueller turns the knob of the safe: 38 right, 6 left, 45 right. *Check Clue HH. Turn to 296.*

311
Wary of the Indians, you walk along the road back to school. The old trees bend their branches in a somber tunnel over your head. A bird calls; you start and wheel around, frightened, to see a quail take off from the underbrush, its wings giving off a distinctive rush as he flies. Although you are safer on the road than in the woods, you could easily be accosted here. For once, you are glad to enter the school's gates and break into a run at the broad drive.

Back in your dormitory, you cannot find Mark. In your room, you notice an envelope protruding from the pages of a book on Mark's desk. Hoping it will tell you something about Mark's whereabouts or the emerald, you dare to open it and read:

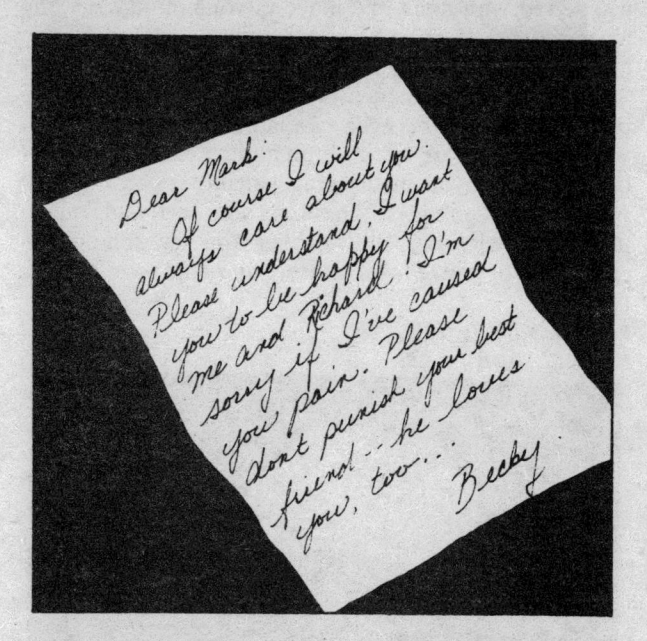

> Dear Mark:
> Of course I will always care about you. Please understand, I want you to be happy for me and Richard. I'm sorry if I've caused you pain. Please don't punish your best friend—he loves you, too...
> Becky

Check Clue H. Mark walks into the room and brushes past you. The note lies on the desk. **Pick a number and add your Artifice bonus:**
- **If 2-6, turn to 199.**
- **If 7-12, turn to 233.**

312

"I'm certain that Joe Miller is blackmailing his brother, Headmaster Mueller," you say.

"That provides a motive," Holmes agrees, "but a very weak one." ***Turn to 305.***

313

You race after Muskrat as he heads toward the cliffs. You follow him behind a large rock, to an opening of a cave. The cave stretches behind a ridge where the rock turns red. Realizing you can go no further without being discovered, you mark the place in your mind, deciding to come back later and explore the cave when Rafferty has gone. *Check Clue AAA*.

You walk back quickly toward where the dart hit the tree. As you head between two large oaks, a pain seizes your chest. You are spun round and round, the treetops turning above you in dizzying kaleidoscope of leaves' shadows and sun's rays. Vines bind your feet, and you are pulled to a clearing. Birds jabber and cry, echoing on either side of you. *Pick a number and add your Artifice bonus:*
- *If 2-8, turn to 157.*
- *If 9-12, turn to 322.*

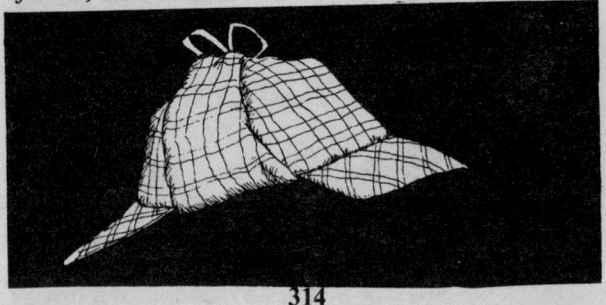

314

The branch cracks as you shimmy back toward the trunk of the tree. You fall to the ground with a thud, your ankle giving way. Looking up, you notice a figure — Bingley's — racing behind the fence. You stand, almost buckling with the pain at your ankle, and hobble toward the woods. *Reduce your Athletics bonus by one for the remainder of this adventure.* As you reach the woods, Bingley opens the gate, and you hide behind a tree. *Pick a number and add your Artifice bonus:*
- *If 2-6, turn to 337.*
- *If 7-12, turn to 145.*

315

You peer through the window. Old man Rafferty and Mueller seem to be arguing a great deal, with Rafferty throwing up his hands in frustration. Then Rafferty waves a newspaper clipping at Mueller — perhaps the article about Mahoney's being hit with a dart. When he shows the headmaster a dart which he removes from his pocket, Mueller turns white.

Then Rafferty takes a black jewel box from his briefcase and leaves it on the desk. In response, Mueller takes letters from his desk drawer and holds them up. Rafferty backs away, leaving the briefcase and jewelry box on the desk, puts on his coat and turns to leave. Mueller shouts after him: "We have a contract!" *Check Clue EE.* **Turn to 185.**

316

"But I've left my money at the school. I will pay you tomorrow," you swear. "I'll sign a note."

Sighing, the man agrees. You sign a note and receive Holmes' letter. **Turn to 180.**

317

The owner and Bingley bicker. The owner reaches beneath the counter and counts out money, which he hands to Bingley. You estimate the roll of bills to be worth 30 pounds! *Check Clue A.*

You race away from the shop as Bingley comes toward the door. By the time you try to follow him again, he is lost in the crowd of hawkers and beggars along the main thoroughfare. Resignedly, make your way to the train station. **Turn to 224.**

318

You study the dart, which has a sharp metal point like that of a fishhook and is stained black with liquid at the tip: curare, from South America? You examine the shaft and a sheaf of paper unrolls. The paper, on examination, is a thin curl of birchbark, with the following symbols on it:

And the words, roughly scribbled:

WATER STONE OURS. TAKE HURT. FIND GIVE.

***Pick a number** and add your Scholarship bonus:*
- *If 2-9, turn to 366.*
- *If 10-12, turn to 345.*

319

You doggedly follow Bingley through a seamy side of London, to Upper Swandham Lane, a filthy alley lurking behind the high wharves which line the north side of the Thames. The smell of opium fumes drift up from the steps which plunge into the dark basements of the buildings along the lane. Richard moves past a gin-shop and enters an old pawn shop, the windows darkened with grime. Old musical instruments, silverware, a tea setting, and brick-a-brack are displayed in the shop windows. You slowly approach and see Richard hand the owner several items, which you strain to discern. ***Pick a number** and add your Observation Bonus:*
- *If 2-7, turn to 234.*
- *If 8-12, turn to 120.*

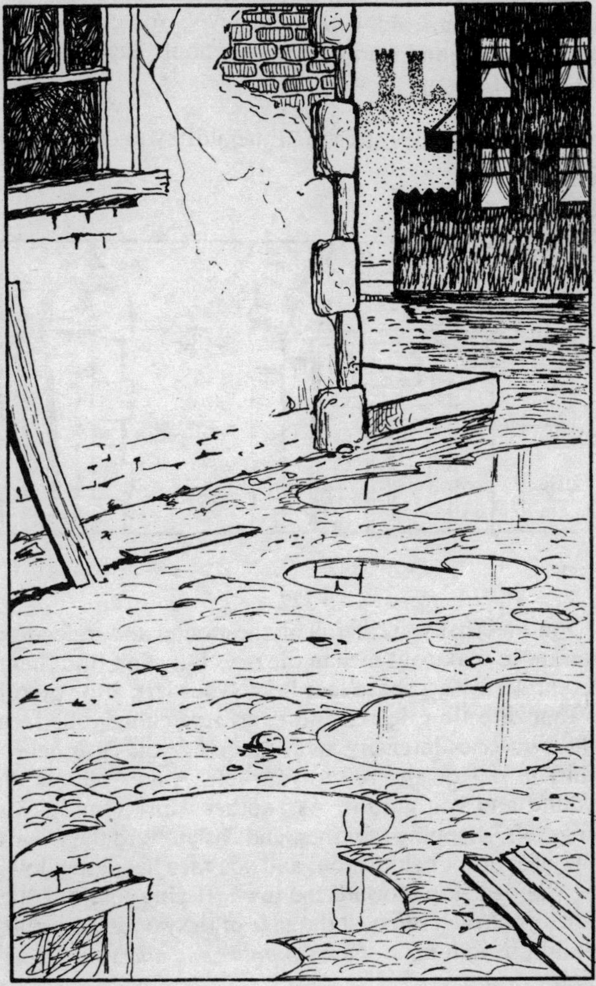

6

320

The jewel gleams blue, not green, and cannot be the Black River Emerald. *Check Clue NN*. You climb down from the tree and hurry back to school. *Turn to 223*.

321

"Richard Bingley stole the Emerald!" you cry. *Turn to 365*.

322

You find that you can roll on the ground and seek cover. You try to make out men in the trees but can't find them. A boulder with a sharp face lies to your left, and you roll in that direction, leaves and twigs scratching your face. The bird cries intensify, as if mocking you. You hear a whirr in the air and roll to your left. A dart pierces the ground and you grab it. As another whirr sounds, you lunge left, snapping the vines, and dash toward the woods. The cries erupt behind you, and you race headlong down the wooded slope toward the town, fleeing for your life. When you reach safety at the edge of the woods, you study the dart in your hand. *Pick a number and add your Observation bonus.*
- *If 2-5, turn to 132.*
- *If 6-12, turn to 318.*

323

"He's after me!" you cry.

"Who's after you?" the train attendant asks with doubtful smile, his florid cheeks puffing out.

Lomax barges through the railway car's doors.

"He is! That man!"

"He does seem in a hurry." Lomax stops and turns away. "Sir!" the attendant calls, as Lomax leaves the car.

"It's all right. Let him go," you say. "We just had a slight misunderstanding. But I'd like to stay close by, if you don't mind."

"Taking on a pretty tough bloke, aren't you? Well, I like a lad with fighting blood in him. If you like, I can show you the engine room."

For the rest of the trip you stay close by the attendant, a gruff, friendly old fellow reeking of stale tobacco. *Turn to 244.*

324

"Muskrat Rafferty stole the Emerald!" you cry. *Turn to 365.*

325

You search for a hidden panel, but it eludes you. Disconsolate, you leave through a window and hurry back to 221B Baker Street to tell Sherlock Holmes all that you have learned. *Turn to 297.*

326

The pattern left by a boot-print catches your eye — parallel horizontal ridges and a W tread on the heel-print. The pattern seems familiar. *Pick a number and add your Observation bonus:*
- *If 2-7, turn to 143.*
- *If 8-12, turn to 191.*

327

Becky turns away, and you cannot hear her.

Suddenly, Mark picks up a stone from ground and flings it toward a tree, saying something about "the one valuable I really cared about." *Check Clue DD.* He mentions class and walks off, not waving to Becky.

You watch as the girl sits on the rim of a stone fountain and weeps. Then she stands, dries her eyes, and runs into the house. Five minutes later, she emerges with a suitcase. On a hunch, you follow her to the train station.
- *If you follow her on the train, turn to 307.*
- *Otherwise, turn to 218.*

328

Answering a knock at the door, you are asked by little Higby-Ross to attend a high tea for your form at the headmaster's house at 4:00 this afternoon. *Pick a number and add your Communications bonus:*
- *If 2-8, turn to 282.*
- *If 9-12, turn to 241.*

329

When you get to the window of the shop, Rafferty is nowhere to be seen. He has somehow left the grocery shop by a different exit.

You enter the shop.

"Can I help you, lad?" the man gruffly asks.

You quickly survey the shop. Tins of vegetables are ranged on shelves along the back wall. The tins of peas catch your eye, one of them lying on its side.

"I've come for some peas," you say.

"On the shelf there."

"Oh, thank you." You take the tipped tin of Braxton's Peas off the shelf. *Pick a number and add your Observation bonus:*
- *If 2-7, turn to 153.*
- *If 8-12, turn to 350.*

330

You approach the safe.
- *If you have checked Clue HH, turn to 228.*
- *Otherwise, turn to 124.*

331

Yes! You have found it! You quickly take the overgrown path up to the cave. ***Turn to 281.***

332

Mr. Holmes takes a deep breath and begins a long explanation of the crime. "Mr. Mueller made a promise to his mother to take care of Joe, his drunkard brother. Relying upon this promise, the brother had moved to town, changed his name to Miller, and lived off the 'charity' of his brother, Headmaster Mueller. To silence his brother, Mueller began embezzling funds from the school. Hoping to regain the money, he made bad investments with school money, which sunk him deeper in debt. As the school's debts mounted, the school itself deteriorated. With the threat of services being cut off and his embezzlement revealed, Mueller seized the chance to recoup the money by stealing the Black River Emerald. When Higby-Ross's music box was stolen, Mueller conducted a search of the rooms, and either then or during one of the school meals — which he attended only infrequently — he discovered the false bottom to Mark's trunk. An amateur magician, he slipped the chain from Mark's neck with slight of hand, when Mark was knocked unconscious on the rugby field. Then he turned to the underworld figure, Mr. Rafferty, whose son Muskrat attended the school, to sell the jewel for their mutual benefit. But when Mahoney's fate was made public in the newspaper, the jewel became too difficult to sell and too dangerous to keep, so Rafferty returned the Emerald to Mueller."

As Holmes pauses to light his pipe, you try to take in all that he has said thus far.

"Mark Avery and Richard Bingley were best friends," Holmes continues, exhaling pale blue smoke. "Mark met Becky Conolly in town and fell in love with her. Through him, she met Richard Bingley, and they fell in love, leaving Mark resentful and bitter. Because Bingley's noble parents did not approve of his marriage to a common girl, young Bingley hid his love for Becky. He sold his valuables and reported them stolen to give her presents."

"That makes sense," you agree.

"Muskrat tried to steal the emerald, as he had stolen other valuables from other students, but failed," Holmes asserts. "His father was working with Mr. Mueller, independently of Muskrat. Oxy wanted the jewel and assumed that Muskrat had stolen it, but he wasn't bright enough to engineer the theft."

Holmes pauses to pull on his pipe, blue smoke ringing his aquiline face, before addressing you directly. "A most singular and curious enigma has come your way, and you have, through your ingenuity and resources, helped to solve the mystery. My congratulations, lad! Ah, and speaking of deductions, that is Watson's tread upon the stairs, if I am not very much mistaken."

Puffing hard, Dr. Watson enters the room and relates that Mueller was found unconscious in the woods behind his house with a dart in his side and an opened jewel box in his hand. He adds that Mark is safe and would like to see you, and that Becky Connoly and Richard Bingley have eloped.

Holmes pulls on the pipe. "Please visit us anytime you happen by Baker Street, Master Rogers, and should another adventure come your way, I shall be most pleased to be of any assistance I can." He lays down the pipe. "And now, gentlemen, I believe Mrs. Hudson requests our attendance at an especially succulent repast." **The End**

333

You stealthily move behind shelves as the man walks the aisles of the shop. Suddenly you are grabbed by your collar from behind. "So we have a thief, have we?" The burly grocer grins. He carries you to the door and boots you into the street. You move off, watching the shop. Minutes later, Rafferty emerges and takes a cab across town, losing you in the traffic. Disconsolate, you walk back to 221B Baker Street to tell Sherlock Holmes all that you have learned. ***Turn to 297.***

334

You cannot reach the horse and scramble back to the cart. ***Turn to 162.***

335

After considerable effort and ingenuity, you reconstruct some of the letter, and read:

...the stone.. tre... hazard to you and to

self as well..........................you bring

..erald home... you wh....

this with utm... secrec.. could come .. you

...that wo.. .nl. .ast both.. in great dan...

.hil. yo..ve the stone wit... e in consider..

..nger. B.. circumspect...closely..

.ecret I have tr.. n you h th. and

. .nt that as an Avery shall merit that

Pick a number *and add your Intuition bonus:*
- *If 2-8, turn to 255.*
- *If 9-12, turn to 186.*

336

You hear Mueller muttering to himself. The handle of the office door turns, and the door creaks open. Realizing that you may be discovered, you move to the door and dash past Mueller, knocking him down. Did he see me, you wonder. You race quickly down the hall and across the campus to your dormitory, where you creep up to your room and crawl into bed with your clothes on. A moment later, trembling with fear, you hear footsteps coming up the stairs, move down the hall and move away. *Turn to 206.*

337

Bingley rushes toward you. You hurry toward the woods, but he catches up to you, hurling you roughly to the ground. *Turn to 262.*

338

You return to 221B Baker Street, hoping that Mr. Holmes and Dr. Watson haven't left. You knock, and stand blushing as Watson opens the door.

"Where the devil have you been off to?" Watson asks. "Most extraordinary, dashing off like that."

"Come in," Holmes says, smiling. "Watson, we have a heavens, he's a Baker Street Irregular at heart. It makes me feel a little easier." As you catch your breath, Holmes reaches for a pipe and tobacco. *Turn to 300.*

339

"My brother will teach you," the drunkard Miller says, his breath reeking. Nausea overwhelms you.

"So you have a great family, eh?" you ask.

"Indeed I do," brags Miller.

"Dukes and earls?" A giggle bubbles up from your lungs.

He grabs your coat. "Watch who you're laughing at."

"Sorry." You pull out a shilling from your pocket. "And would you be interested in having some refreshment?"

"I wouldn't mind," Miller says.

"Tell me about your relatives."

"Eh, what's that? What are you trying to do?" Miller scowls at you threateningly. *Pick a number and add your Communication bonus:*
- *If 2-8, turn to 149.*
- *If 9-12, turn to 183.*

340

Leaving Holmes' flat, you reach the main thoroughfare and, with a jolt of recognition, notice Richard Bingley moving through the crowd. He marches off down a crowded side street.
- *If you follow him, turn to 319.*
- *Otherwise, turn to 224.*

341

Neither Holmes nor Watson has returned when you arrive at 221B Baker Street. You leave a message for Holmes, recounting what you have learned so far and asking for Holmes' help, as you would rather not go to the police. Then you hurry back to Belton School, wondering how to explain your absence. *Turn to 218.*

342

You hear the words "money" and "emerald" clearly, and something about a "stone." Then Oxy snarls, and advances on Muskrat, his great frame completely blocking the escape of the cringing Muskrat.

"I want that emerald!" Oxy snarls. "Cheatin' me again — " From behind Oxy music suddenly arises, music like chimes, as perfect and elegant as snowflakes. Oxy pauses and gradually grows calm, mesmerized like a beast by the chiming music. You catch a quick motion as Muskrat slides past him and races toward the cave door. Pulling back, you flatten yourself against the cliff wall. *Check Clue BB. Pick a number and add your Artifice bonus:*
- *If 2-8, turn to 114.*
- *If 9-12, turn to 277.*

343

Your arm thobs with pain, your breathing is rapid and shallow, and your muscles go limp. *Reduce your Athletics bonus by 1 for the remainder of this adventure. Turn to 370.*

344

You get a flash of insight — the Case of the Speckled Band! You get on your knees and discover that the grate beneath your bed goes to the room below. If you can find the room above or below Rafferty's, you can eavesdrop on them. Since Rafferty's room is on the top floor near yours, you must find the room below his. You walk down the hall, counting the rooms from his to the main stairway.

Downstairs you count the rooms and come to the door of room 215. *Pick a number and add your Communication bonus:*
- *If 2-6, turn to 360.*
- *If 7-12, turn to 213.*

345

The second panel shows a figure casting a dart at a figure holding a diamond shaped object that glows: the Emerald! The third panel show the figure holding the emerald and the dart as well; apparently, he has conquered the man who had the emerald and possesses the emerald himself. The fourth panel shows him above wavy lines, which indicate a stream of water: the Black River? The first panel identifies the emerald with the Black River, indicating that the Black River Indians are the true owners of the emerald.

The words give the message: *The water stone (the emerald) is ours. We will hurt those who take it. Find the stone and give it to us. Turn to 366.*

346

You inch closer to the entrance of the cave. *Pick a number and add your Artifice bonus:*
- *If 2-8, turn to 178.*
- *If 9-12, turn to 117.*

347

Their voices are low; you cannot quite understand them. As they embrace, you notice a pendant with a stone hanging from a chain around Becky's neck. *Check Clue N.* You creep forward on the branch. A cracking sound comes from behind you; the branch is breaking! *Pick a number and add your Athletics bonus:*
- *If 2-6, turn to 211.*
- *If 7-12, turn to 314.*

348

Holmes pulls on his pipe. "I can understand how you might suspect him. My suspicions lay in that direction as well. However, have you considered all the relevant clues of the case? For example, the fact that the food at the school had been getting worse for some time? That the school spared using gas for the lamps, even cancelling study hall? Or indeed, that the school itself has been deteriorating for some time? Tell me all you can, young man, pertaining to the case, and with what I have discovered from my own sources, let me see if I can explain this singular mystery to you."

You relate to Mr. Holmes all the pertinent details of the case that you can recall as he smokes a bowl of shag tobacco. When you have finished, the detective takes a deep breath.

"Your school's headmaster, Mr. Mueller made a promise to his mother to take care of Joe, his drunkard brother," Holmes resumes, exhaling a stream of blue smoke. "Relying upon this promise, the brother had moved to town, changed his name to Miller, and lived off Mr. Mueller. Trying to buy Joe Miller's silence, Mueller began embezzling funds from the school. Hoping to regain the money, he made bad investments with school money, which put him further in debt. The school's bills mounted, and the school deteriorated from neglect. With the threat of services being cut off and his embezzlement revealed, Mr. Mueller seized the chance to recoup the money by stealing the Black River Emerald. When Higby-Ross's music box was stolen, Mueller conducted a search of the rooms and either then or during one of the school meals — which he attended only infrequently — he discovered the false bottom to Mark Avery's trunk. An amateur magician, Mueller slipped the chain from Mark's neck with slight of hand, when Mark was knocked unconscious on the rugby field. He then turned to the underworld figure, Mr. Rafferty, whose son Muskrat attended the school, to sell the jewel for their mutual benefit. But when Mahoney's fate was made public, the Emerald became too difficult to sell and too dangerous to keep, so Rafferty returned it to Mueller. Mueller then tried to escape, but, too greedy, he took the jewel with him, and met his fate at the hands of the Indians."

You nod, thus far following Holmes' deductions.

"Mark Avery and Richard Bingley were best friends," Holmes goes on, rarely looking at you. "Mark met Becky Conolly in town and fell in love with her. Through him, she met Richard Bingley, and they fell in love, leaving Mark resentful and bitter. Because Richard Bingley's parents did not approve of his marriage to a common girl, he arranged to elope with her to Paris. Young Bingley sold all his valuables and reported them stolen, to give Becky presents and to provide the money to make their escape with."

"I see," you say, amazed at Holmes' thorough grasp of the facts.

"Muskrat tried to steal the emerald, as he had stolen other valuables from other students, but failed," Holmes surmises, staring out the window. "As it happens, his father was scheming with Mr. Mueller, independently of Muskrat, to steal the same jewel. Oxy also coveted the Emerald and assumed that Muskrat had stolen it, but he wasn't bright enough to engineer the theft of your friend's treasure. Ah, and speaking of companions, that is Watson's tread upon the stairs, if I am not very much mistaken, to tell us more of the fate of the jewel."

Out of breath, Dr. Watson enters the room and relates that Headmaster Mueller was found unconscious in the woods behind his house with a dart in his side and an opened jewel box in his hand. He adds that Mark is safe and would like to see you, and that Becky Connoly and Richard Bingley have eloped.

Holmes takes a puff on his pipe, blue smoke ringing his aquiline face. "I should not be too discouraged, young Master Rogers. A most singular and curious enigma has come your way which few, lacking my abilities, could have solved."

Watson lays a friendly arm on your shoulder. "How often, David, I have been the recipient of such consolations! We are companions, lad, and I should be pleased to call you friend. Please visit us anytime you happen by Baker Street."

Rising to his feet, Holmes pulls on his pipe. "Let me also extend that invitation, Master Rogers. And should another adventure come your way, I shall be delighted to be of any assistance I can." He lays down the pipe. "And now, gentlemen, I believe Mrs. Hudson requests our attendance at an especially succulent repast." **The End**

349

You dash amid the trees, rushing past them with the same skill that you use to elude defenders on the rugby field. You're almost keeping pace with him! Half-naked, the man is painted in bright colors, yellow and green and black in a pattern of rushing water. A loincloth painted with the same pattern covers his waist. You follow him between two great oak trees.

Suddenly, pain seizes your chest. You are spun round and round, the treetops turning above you in dizzying kaleidoscope of leaves' shadows and sun's rays. Vines bind your feet, and you are pulled to a clearing. Birds jabber and cry on either side of you. *Pick a number and add your Artifice bonus:*
- *If 2-8, turn to 157.*
- *If 9-12, turn to 322.*

350

Behind the tipped tin of peas on the shelf you notice a door handle, and then a vertical crack of light in the wall. *Check Clue GG. Turn to 153.*

351

"I haven't got the money," says Muskrat, cringing.

"Then where's the emerald?" Oxy yells.

"I don't have the emerald."

"Liar! Don't give me that. It was you stole it."

"I didn't," Muskrat insists. "I don't have it."

Oxy seethes, shaking his fist in the smaller boy's face. "You told me you stole it."

"I told you I stole something. But not the emerald. Oh, I tried, of course.."

"What did you steal?" Oxy asks, confused.

From beneath a blanket hidden under the dirt, Muskrat pulls out a music box.

"You can have this," Musrat says, handing it to Oxy. "It's real valuable."

"What do I want with this?" Oxy snaps. "I want my bleedin' money or the stone — or your blood. You have that stone." Oxy advances on the smaller boy, his great frame completely blocking the escape of the cringing Muskrat. "I want that emerald! Cheatin' me again — " From behind them comes music, music like chimes, as beautiful and elegant as snowflakes. Oxy shifts slowly, gradually calming himself, mesmerized like a beast by the chiming music. You catch a quick motion as Muskrat slides past him and races toward the cave door. Pulling back, you flatten yourself against the cliff wall. *Check Clues AA, T and U.* **Pick a number and add your Artifice bonus:**
- *If 2-7, turn to 114.*
- *If 8-12, turn to 277.*

352

Stunned, you reach for Holmes' pipe, now filled with old socks. ***Turn to 352.***

353

As you're walking through the woods, you hear bird cries. You pick up speed, but the bird cries keep pace with you. A dart hits the tree just ahead! You shift to your left, and a dart strikes the tree to your left. The bird cries intensify. Running, you catch your foot on the ground and stumble forward. The leaves crackle beside you as you slide along the forest floor. Suddenly, two small dark figures appear between the trees. Bird calls sound behind you, and when you wheel around, the figures have gone.

As you stand, you hear the bird cries further off in the forest, as if calling you.

- *If you follow the calls, **turn to 187**.*
- *Otherwise, **turn to 181**.*

354

The lock will not spring; you cannot enter Mueller's office. You hear someone approaching and flee. ***Turn to 174.***

Miller lunges for the coin, but you pull your hand away and hold the coin behind your back.

"My brother will beat you senseless if he finds you been treating me this way," Miller says.

"Your brother — who is he?"

"Give you a few whacks, he will. Give all you schoolboys a whack."

You laugh. "Your brother's connected with Belton School?"

"Not just connected, man. Not just connected," Miller says, raising an eyebrow. "He's the head of the bloody place. He's the Headmaster."

"You drink too much. It gives you strange dreams."

"I can prove it! Why do you think I live in this stinking town? Gives me what he can. It's only fair. Wouldn't be in this condition, if it hadn't been for me mum. Always favorin' him, always givin' him money, buyin' him his fancy education — and she sends me to work. Well, who's payin who? Who's supportin' who now? Only fair. Now hand me over the shilling."

You hand Miller the coin. *Deduct the shilling from your Character Record.* His teeth, etched with brown decay, grin at you as he pushes open the door of pub. You head to the post office, wondering if what he said could be true. *Check Clue D. Turn to 283.*

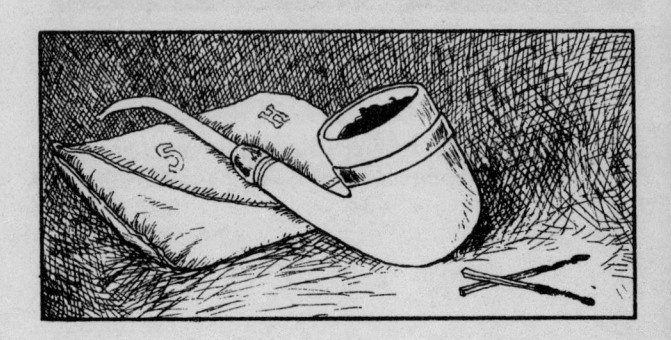

356

The note is almost illegible. *Pick a number and add your Intuition bonus:*
- *If 2-5, turn to 255.*
- *If 6-9, turn to 303.*
- *If 10-12, turn to 247.*

> matter at hand has ... ... the ... ...
> at I have tol... you. Certain e... ... made y...
> ssession o... ...he sto... ...treme haz... ...o you... ...nd to
> yself as ...ell. It ... ...f utmost imp...ance tha... ...ou bri...
> ...erald...home u... ...you wh... ...e o... Frid... ...nd th...
> u do this wi... ...utm... ...secre... ...could come to you...
> ...uld, b... ... wo... ...nly cast both of us in grea... ...dan...
> will explain wh... ...I se... you... ...o not mean... ...arm yo...
> ...whil... u... ...e the stone wit... ... ...re in conside...
> ...nger. ...cumspec... ...and th... ...t close..., and ke...
> ...secre... ...I have place... my tru... ...n you with th... ...ar...
> ...fident that as an Avery... ...shall merit that...

357

As you make your way between two large oaks, pain seizes your chest. You are spun round and round, the treetops turning above you in dizzying kaleidoscope of leaves' shadows and sun's rays. Vines bind your feet, and you are pulled to a clearing. Birds jabber and cry, echoing on either side of you. *Pick a number and add your Artifice bonus:*
- *If 2-8, turn to 157.*
- *If 9-12, turn to 322.*

358

You put out your arm, and the shovel's blade hits your forearm, which goes weak with a pain. Oxy brings his leg behind yours and topples with you onto the floor. You feel something give in your back. *Reduce your Athletics bonus by 1 point for the remainder of this adventure.* Oxy sits on you, pinning you to the floor, Muskrat leering above him.

The door opens. Mark Avery leans against the doorjamb, and relief floods over you. Mark pushes off from the doorjamb. "What seems to be happening here?"

"I think we've found our thief," Oxy says. "We found him filchin' from my bureau."

"I was trying to find the emerald," you cry.

"Thieving is what he was," Muskrat whines.

Oxy comes down on you. "He's the filcher who's been taking all our watches and the like — and your emerald, I'll wager."

Mark approaches and stands over you. "Well, well, so he is a thief after all."

"I was trying to find the emerald," you stammer. "I figured maybe Oxy stole it."

"And maybe I'm the king of Persia," Mark sneers, his boot swinging toward you, jabbing you. It all makes sense. A hawker couldn't sell the jewel here—not with my father's power and connections. But take it out of the country, take it home across the ocean to America and—" The boot jabs you as though on a pendulum. He smiles. "You're pretty smooth for such a studious lad, Rogers. I give him everything, even invite him to my home—" He wipes his boot on your uniform jacket. "That's a very nice jacket you've got. Shame to muss it up. Must have cost you a pretty penny. You should learn to take care of nice things. You like them well enough, for someone who can't afford them." He wipes the other boot across your jacket. "Give him a pretty coat like this, and he can't even keep the thing clean," Mark says to the grinning pair. His boot, the W tread on the heel, swings toward you and catches you in the ribs. Muskrat grins above Oxy. The door creaks open, and Master Dirkforth, the mathematics teacher and floor supervisor, comes in.

"What's going on here?" he demands.

Oxy gets up, freeing you. You spring to your feet and dash past the bewildered Master Dirkforth.

Later that night, after chapel, you wait in the lavatory until everyone else is asleep, and creep quietly to your bed, muttering a prayer of thanks. *Turn to 204.*

359

Miller grabs the coin and moves away from you, laughing through his cigar stub. His teeth, etched with brown decay, grin at you as he pushes open the door of the pub. Annoyed, you head to the post office. *Deduct the shilling from your Character Record. Turn to 283.*

360

You knock on the door and hear a high murmur beyond. Entering, you find a boy crying — Vincent Higby-Ross from the fourth form. "What's the matter?" you ask, moving under the grate in the ceiling over in the corner.

"Someone stole my music box!" Vincent cries. Tears stream down his cheeks. "It had a beautiful horse of gold on one side, and a silver carriage on the other." Murmurs come from upstairs, but you can't make them out.
out.

Higby-Ross wails. "I can't get to sleep at night! If I don't sleep, I'll never study and I'll never get out of here! And Da' will never let me come home!"

"Why can't you sleep?" you ask, trying to calm him.

"You promise not to laugh?"

The angry voice of the old man comes from above, but you can't decipher the words. "I promise I won't laugh."

"That's the only way I could get to sleep — by playing the box. We used to play the box at home. I pretend I'm home again, and, and, I hate it here. And if I can't pass my exams I'll never get home!"

"We all hate it here," you say, trying to console him. The conversation upstairs ends. You abandon the your quest and return to your room, determined to keep an eye out for trouble. *Turn to 216.*

361

You stumble to the Railway Station to catch the train to school. At the ticket window, handsome and vain Richard Bingley greets you with "Old sport!" and tells you he's been to see a play. He smiles haughtily at you and says: "I hear our great friend has turned on you too." His thin lips twist bitterly beneath the Roman nose and the high aristocratic brow of his family line.

"I suppose so", you say. "Mark thinks I stole the emerald."

"Hard cheese, old bean."

You try to figure out if he is mocking you. "He never did tell me why you had a falling out."

"And neither will I," Bingley says, his aquiline features hardening into marble. "But I knew all along he would pay." He laughs bitterly and takes a puff of his thin Galliardi cigar, which he smokes, flaunting the school rules, in front of other students and teachers alike, as if daring them to punish their wealthiest and most famous student. "I just knew he'd pay. It's enough to make one religious. Hey! Pretend you don't know me on the train — I have a girl!" He laughs again as the train chugs past the others into the station in a gush of smoke and steam. *Turn to 293.*

362

You strike out against him with your fist. Mark falls back against the far wall, and, stunned, stumbles from the room, cursing you. You stand and pick up the crumpled sheet beside the fire's glowing embers. Slumping into a chair, you smooth out the burned sheet on the desk, and try to read it. *Turn to 356.*

363

The boys run through the woods, probably toward the cave, ducking and weaving, and you cannot keep pace. Where did they go?
- *If you checked Clue T, turn to 182.*
- *Otherwise, pick a number and add your Intuition bonus:*
  - *If 2-8, turn to 101.*
  - *If 9-12, turn to 182.*

7

364

Headmaster Mueller, an amateur magician, comes on stage in a puff of smoke. In the audience, a student lets out a large burp and everyone laughs. Calling for silence, Mueller asks for volunteers. Higby-Ross raises his hand and goes up. Mueller then puts a gold chain around his neck, and while doing so, surreptitiously steals the boy's wallet. As Mueller hands the shaken boy his wallet to great applause, the headmaster distracts him with a curious circular motion of his hands. While having him pick a card from a deck, Mueller pauses: "Oh, is this yours?" he says, and produces the gold chain. Higby-Ross checks for the gold chain around his neck, but it is gone. The boys cheer. "And you seem to want me to keep this, too," Mueller gloats, as he hands Higby-Ross his wallet yet again. *Check Clue X*.

A crash is heard off stage. Then Joe Miller stumbles onto the stage, drunk, and shouts: "A few bob! A bloke needs a few bob!" The stage lights seem to stagger him. A man starved for attention, he drinks it in, as if to guzzle it. He mumbles some curse drunkenly. *Pick a number and add your Observation bonus:*
- *If 2-7, turn to 109.*
- *If 8-12, turn to 371.*

365

Suddenly, a strange bird call from outside freezes the Indians' attention; they hurl you and Mark to the floor and slip from the room. The woods echoes with the clatter of bird cries. Mark tells you he is fine, and bewildered, you decide to hurry to 221B Baker Street.

"Perhaps Mr. Holmes can make sense of this mess," you tell Mark as you run out the door. *Turn to 202.*

366

You pocket the dart and the note, and stride purposefully toward the village of Belton. *Check Clue M. Turn to 265.*

4

367

You are unconscious and hurt. *Reduce your Intuition Bonus by 1 for the remainder of this adventure. Turn to 188.*

368

When you regain your senses, Mrs. Hudson stands over you. You find yourself in a bed in Holmes' flat.

"Poor lad," Mrs. Hudson exclaims. Holmes sits in his chair, blue smoke curling up from his clay pipe.

"Our young friend will be fine, Mrs. Hudson," says the detective.

"Brave lad," she remarks.

"Perhaps too much so," Holmes says.

Mrs Hudson smiles over you. "Would you care for some biscuits?"

Your head aches, and your arm thobs with pain. "But how — "

Holmes smiles. "I dispatched Watson to lend a hand. Your friend Mark Avery found you in the woods, a bit worse for wear from the Indians. He's been most helpful and solicitous. Watson brought you here under his superlative care and has returned to Belton to assist in returning the stone to its rightful owners." He draws on his pipe. "But perhaps you can solve the mystery for us," says Holmes, the blue smoke ringing his aquiline face. ***Turn to 202.***

369

You notice the edge of a rug beneath the dirt and pull it. Below the rug lies a chest; you open the hinged lid. Inside you find Higby-Ross's music box. It has a golden horse on one side, and an elegant silver carriage on the other. But you cannot find the Emerald. Disappointed, you return to school. *Check Clue U. Turn to 353.*

370

Perspiration drenches your clothes. You find that you can roll toward cover and do so. You try to make out men in the trees but can't find them. Using your teeth, you pull the dart out, causing a piercing stab of pain.

A boulder with a sharp face lies to your left, and you roll in that direction, leaves and twigs scratching your face. Your shoulder aches so sharply that you almost lose consciousness. Your hands find the boulder's edge and you cut the vines, listening intently. You stand, weak and dazed, and retrieve the dart. ***Pick a number and add your Observation bonus:***
* *If 2-8, turn to 132.*
* *If 9-12, turn to 318.*

371

"What do you think of a man that won't even help his bleedin' brother?" Joe Miller cries to the audience.

Headmaster Mueller turns to the students, intoning: "Here, my young friends, is a lesson in dissolute living. Work hard, lads, and you can achieve anything in the world." The fabric of his coat moves, and Mueller palms a pound note from his pocket. "Lie about and play games, and you shall find yourself living in the gutter. Thank you, sir, for providing this valuable lesson to our students." Mueller shakes Joe Miller's hand, giving him the pound note and ushering him off-stage. *Check Clue Y. Turn to 226.*

You push the charging Oxy back with your legs; he crashes against the dresser with a curse. You elbow Muskrat and run into the hall and down the stairs.

Back in your room, you lock the door and catch your breath, thinking: if Oxy took the Black River Emerald, where is it? You fall asleep reading Shakespeare's "Othello." *Turn to 204.*

SHERLOCK HOLMES SOLO MYSTERIES

SHERLOCK HOLMES SOLO MYSTERIES present a series of living novels designed for solitary play. Each gamebook is an original mystery which the reader/detective must solve (with a bit of help from Holmes and Watson). Since the reader's choices affect his ability to unravel the mystery, SHERLOCK HOLMES SOLO MYSTERIES can be played again and again! So grab your magnifying glass and prepare to match wits with the master sleuth! SHERLOCK HOLMES SOLO MYSTERIES .... having fun was never so elementary!

Produced & Distributed by
IRON CROWN
ENTERPRISES INC.
P.O. Box 1605
Charlottesville, VA 22902

MIDDLE-EARTH ROLE PLAYING™

MIDDLE-EARTH ROLE PLAYING (MERP) is a Fantasy Role Playing Game system perfect for novices as well as experienced gamers! Based on THE HOBBIT and THE LORD OF THE RINGS, MERP provides the structure and framework for role playing in the greatest fantasy setting of all time....J.R.R. Tolkien's Middle-earth! MERP is well supported by a wide variety of game aids, Campaign Modules, Adventure Supplements, and Ready-to-Run Adventures. MIDDLE-EARTH ROLE PLAYING....a world apart!

Produced & Distributed by
IRON CROWN
ENTERPRISES INC.
P.O. Box 1605
Charlottesville, VA 22902

Space Master™

Now you can adventure in space with I.C.E.'s Science-Fiction Role Playing Game system! Experience life aboard a deep space Outstation, become embroiled in the constant conflict between the ruling Houses of the Core Provinces, or travel to the frontier in search of vital resources. SPACE MASTER includes guidelines for a wide range of technologies — from tomorrow to the far future. Its rules cover professions, races, cultures, settings, starship construction, personal and vehicular combat, and much more! SPACE MASTER....
the challenge of the future awaits!

Produced & Distributed by
IRON CROWN
ENTERPRISES INC.
P.O. Box 1605
Charlottesville, VA 22902

Rolemaster™

I.C.E.'s advanced Fantasy Role Playing Game system. ROLEMASTER is a complete set of the most advanced, realistic, and sophisticated rules available. The flexibility of the system allows it to be used wholly or in part. ROLEMASTER's component parts include: CHARACTER LAW & CAMPAIGN LAW, ARMS LAW & CLAW LAW, and SPELL LAW. Each of these can be used separately to improve the realism of most major FRP systems! Now you can add detail to your fantasy gaming without sacrificing playability! ROLEMASTER. . . . a cut above the rest!

Produced & Distributed by
IRON CROWN
ENTERPRISES INC.
P.O. Box 1605
Charlottesville, VA 22902

WE NEED YOUR FEEDBACK!

PLEASE HELP US DO A BETTER JOB ON FUTURE BOOKS BY ANSWERING SOME OR ALL OF THE FOLLOWING QUESTIONS & SENDING YOUR REPLIES TO I.C.E.:

I purchased this book at _____
_____(name of store).

The name of this book is _____
_____.

I am (male/female) _____, and _____ years of age. I am in the _____ grade in school.

I live in a (small, medium, large) _____ town/city.

My favorite magazine is _____.

I heard about this gamebook through_____
_____ (a friend, a family member, an advertisement, other _____).

The one thing I like the *most* about this Sherlock Holmes Solo Mystery is _____
_____
_____.

The one thing I like the *least* about this Sherlock Holmes Solo Mystery is _____
_____
_____.

Send all feedback replies to:

IRON CROWN ENTERPRISES
P.O. BOX 1605, DEPT., SH
CHARLOTTESVILLE, VA. 22902